Very Good Butter

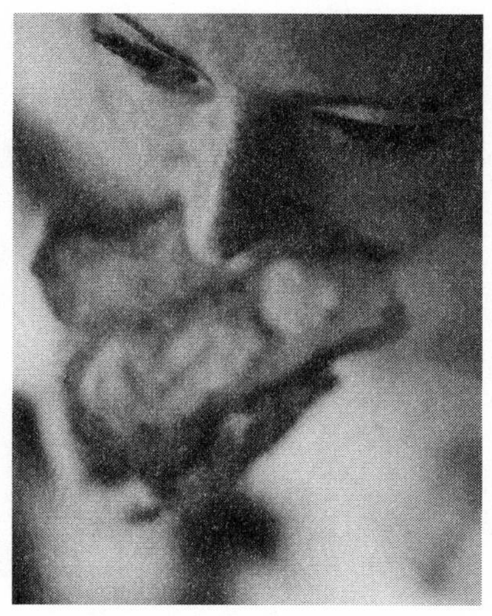

Very Good Butter

STORIES BY JOHN LAVERY

ECW PRESS

CANADIAN CATALOGUING IN PUBLICATION DATA

Lavery, John, 1949 Dec. 31–
Very good butter

A misFit book
ISBN 1-55022-411-5

I. Title

PS8573.A845V47 2000 C813'.6 C00-930442-8
PR9199.3.L336V47 2000

A misFit book edited by Michael Holmes
Cover and text design by Tania Craan
Cover photo by Tony Stone Images
Layout by Mary Bowness
Printed by Veilleux Impression à Demande

Distributed in Canada by General Distribution Services,
325 Humber Blvd., Toronto, Ontario M9W 7C3

Published by ECW PRESS
2120 Queen Street East, Suite 200,
Toronto, Ontario, M4E 1E2
www.ecw.ca/press

The publication of *Very Good Butter* has been generously supported by The Canada Council, the Ontario Arts Council, and the Government of Canada through the Book Publishing Industry Development Program. Canadä

CONTENTS

Acknowledgements

The author would like to acknowledge, gratefully, Canada's many literary journals, and the work they do in publishing so many fine writers. The stories in this collection were first published as follows: "Manon and My Man Jack" in *Quarry*, "The Premier's New Pyjamas" in *Prism international*, "The Breeze Being Needed" in *Prism international*, "The Lactose-Intolerant Daughter" in *Prism international*, "You, Judith Kamada" in *The Antigonish Review*, "The Household Cup" in *Grain*, "Naming Darkness" in *Fiddle-head*, "The Walnut Shell" in *Quarry*, and "See the River Lit Up with Tears" in *Grain*. "Naming Darkness" was reprinted in *Coming Attractions 99* (Oberon Press).

The manuscript for *Very Good Butter* was completed with the assistance of the Canada Council.

aux chefs de bataillon-on-on

sans vous, on n'aurait jamais eu de mes nouvelles

MANON AND MY MAN JACK

How did Jack and I meet?

That's the essential mystery of any couple, isn't it. How they meet.

We met . . . I don't remember how we first met, if we ever did first meet. I received a telephone call from Jack one day. A long time ago now, of course. In France. Lyon. Where I grew up. He identified himself, he said we had been introduced to each other on such and such an evening at such and such a place, and he asked me out. I told him I didn't have the faintest recollection of having met him, which I didn't, and, despite his English-Canadian accent which gave me the impression, then, that he was talking to me through falling snow, I hung up.

He phoned me again the next day, and the next, and the next, and so on. Always very pleasant. Always with the same strong smell of winter in his voice. And always with an undercurrent of such exasperating determination that eventually I said alright, al*right*, I have to go to Besançon for a day, my train's leaving tonight at 9:42, I'll be at the Café de la Gare at nine, nine-fifteen.

I didn't go to the Café de la Gare, I didn't have time.

I spent that night in Besançon, the next night as well, and I returned to Lyon early the following morning, about seven I think.

Now this is the interesting part. The essential mystery. All the time I was away, whether or not I was willing to admit it to myself, an image of a man waiting in a train station flickered in my head. He was sitting on a wooden bench, in those days there were just wooden benches, he stood up and wrapped his black coat more tightly around himself, he stuffed his hands more deeply into his pockets, he sat down again. Over and over he did this, waiting.

And when I got off the train in Lyon, you see, I looked around crossly and consulted my watch as though I were expecting someone to meet me, and then I went into a telephone booth. And there I sat, having dialled my own number, mouthing words into the buzzing receiver, until I turned around and there he was, Jack, looking at me. I was astonished. Not because I knew he had been waiting. But because it was not him. He was completely different. He was Jack but he was not the man in my head. He was not wearing a black, or any other coat. He did not resemble his voice. He did not look pleasant, or healthy. He did not have snow in his eyes. He was formless, paunchy, he looked cruel, he held his mouth open, and he smelled sour, like winter vegetables left out on the counter too long.

I think the idea of the stranger is a man's idea. Men push their hands out through the invisible stranger's coat-of-many-colours they wear in order to shake the hand poking out from the opposite stranger's coat. They like to coat themselves with the idea of the stranger the way they like to coat women with the idea of beauty. They make perfect strangers out of the women they make beautiful.

Women see the stranger as a detonation of possibilities, don't they? They measure the presence of a stranger the way they measure the interval between a flash of lightning and its thunderclap. One paper guitar, two paper guitars, three paper guitars. They listen, however timidly, stupidly, for the biggun, the saviour.

Now I was perfectly willing to accept Jack as my sour-smelling saviour for what, the morning? The week? A lifetime? Two lifetimes? But why? Why submit to fat fate? Why do what destiny tells you to do? Why let the oracles push you around like Oedipus-puss-puss? He should have just sat tight, and he'd have been fine.

He looked so cold, Jack did. I did feel like giving him my coat.

I stepped out of the booth, turned, and walked away.

And Jack followed me. I hadn't thought of that. Why hadn't I thought of that? He was behind me. If I hurried, he would hurry. If I swerved, he would swerve. If I scratched my head and stood on one foot, he would scratch his head and stand on one foot. He was behind me, he had blown a poison dart into my shoulder, I would soon begin to stagger and drool.

Should I get a taxi? I thought. Before I drop. Climb on a

bus? Hide in the wc? Talk to the people? There were so many, but they were all in a train station, and I, I was running over the bleached savanah with its wrinkled bushlets and shimmering grass, my shoulder festering, my man Jack bearing down behind me, sour-smelling, slipping down his sarbacane another poison dart.

I should have just sat tight, or so I thought.

But then I stepped outside and crashed into the glass sunlight, a thousand plexi-pieces broke over me, destiny, as you know, takes so many forms, and as I stood there blinking into this blizzard of light, it was as if destiny took me by the elbows, two of his henchmen perhaps, his bullish, sunny thugs, and they said walk, and I said let go of me first, and then I did walk, in their company but under my own steam, very stern and tall, downhill along the sidewalk to the Hôtel Viotte, past the floral sofas in the front room to the desk, and I said:

"Une chambre, s'il vous plaît. Qui ne donne pas sur la rue."

I heard Jack enter and sit down in one of the floral sofas.

"Non, je ne prends pas le petit déjeuner."

His breathing was dry and very heavy. I glanced at him as I filled in the registration card. He did not look well, he was holding himself very stiffly, as though he were wounded in the side.

"Numéro 7 vous avez dit?" I said too loudly, so Jack would hear.

Yes, yes, room number seven, at the back, the telephone could not be used to make long distance calls, one must first call the desk, the bathroom was on the landing, one must clean the tub afterwards if one took a bath.

I turned, pressing the key into my warm, waxy palm, and looked at my man Jack. He was in an unnatural position, his knees strangely bent, his pelvis pushed forward, his head resting heavily on the back of the sofa. His eyes might have been observing a spider on the ceiling, had they been open.

Which they were not. My man Jack had fallen fast asleep.

Yes, I fell asleep. I had spent two nights in the station. I watched all the passengers getting out of fourteen trains that came in from Besançon.

When the hotel owner woke me up brutally and threw me out, I was nauseated by the need to sleep. I nearly wept, so vivid was the heat of the sun heckling me, so intense the whining of the air in my ears.

And when, finally, I reached my apartment, I slept a flat, lusterless sleep, beneath a crust of hard dreams through which I broke from time to time to find myself in a room so relentlessly familiar it too was a dream, and I scuttled back down my sleep-hole, and curled myself around my stone.

When I woke I felt as though I had been scrubbed by wire brushes, as though I had eaten a pound of ash.

Saint Augustine said this: O madness, that cannot manage to love men with kindness. Foolish man, who cannot manage to live his plain, human hardship without exaggerated suffering.

Foolish Jack Smith, I thought to myself. Manon seemed so far away now, on the other side of my sleep. Ay-yay. Having played a hundred and thirty-one bars more or less perfectly, it hardly seemed tempting to start all over again because of a slip-up in bar one-thirty-two. Enough of this wobbly, Romantic tune. Time to tackle another piece, something disciplined, Dorian. There are, thought I, bedsheets to be crumpled behind any number of dusty, shuttered windows.

I was miffed that he had fallen asleep. Muffled. I hurried out of the hotel, wanting to cry. I hate being made to want to cry.

If he phones me again, I thought to myself, I won't answer. I'll have the number changed.

You will have noticed the pinhole in my logic. The bubble in my glassy vanity.

I never did have to have the number changed.

And, soon enough, I forgot Jack.

However, if, during the next three years or so, I rigorously maintained my resolve not to dial Manon's telephone number, she, nevertheless, rarely stopped piping in my ears with her eccentric, finch's voice. Even as I buried my brains in every convenient alcove where love was a-rub, ran down every round-shouldered Fay that diverted my attentions, Manon beat at my head like a sweet-nosed bat. Even as I left every Queen Mab I could slouching against her bed's headboard, as I tried miserably to squirm out of my atrocious fantasies and regain the Peas-blossom melting in my hands, Manon whinnied at me, from her lake-lair, her kelpie's lament.

She did not stop. She stepped out of the phone booth, turned, and walked away from me. Over and over. Her bay, baleen hair swaying, irised.

Now then, as it happened, I was, at the time, the stage

manager of a small orchestra made up of student musicians playing for experience and for travel. I drove the bus, set up the chairs and music stands, maintained a stock of scores, reeds, pads, flute springs, viola strings, aspirins, ice-packs, and so on.

We were in Turin. The hall was located in an unfinished office tower, awe-inspiring by our standards, so new it made me sneeze, full of chrome, gilt-edged glass, and dead-leaf carpeting. During the first part of our concert, the French horn player (there was only one) took his instrument apart several times, looked through it, shook it, blew it out. At the intermission, he told me there was something stuck inside, so I climbed up on the stage to have a look, and boom! The horn exploded. It blew me right off the stage. Most of me. My left leg was left behind and, fortunately, my soul was left in a state of complete oblivion.

I have always been ashamed of my emotional resilience. I would naturally prefer to be thought of as dancing sadly behind the steam of summer fountains, rather than bundling efficiently through the icy metropolis-mist wrapped in my ten-foot scarf. But I am what I am. At my best in bad weather.

It is that I savour my emotions. I do not feed my soul to them.

So, as I say, I forgot Jack. Until, one day, three years later, the phone rang:

"Madame Manon Joly?"

"Oui."

"Vous connaissez peut-être, Madame Joly, un certain Smeeze? Jacques Smeeze?"

Smeeze? No, I didn't know anybody whose last name was Smeeze. I hope I never do.

"No, madame? You are sure? Jacques Smeeze. A Canadian."

And then, you see, then, in that instant, I covered all the furniture in my last three years of memories with old sheets, and I repainted every room. I opened every window, so the birds too could choke on the white reek of fresh, latex, semi-gloss. And in the middle of the living room, there he was, sitting awkwardly, unshaven, his pelvis pushed forward, observing, even as he slept, a spider on the ceiling. In that instant I inculcated my man Jack with every sort of charm and sun-bursting quality. I redecorated his conversation, perfected the non-paradise out of which he had not even dropped me. Destiny, as I say, takes too many forms, the most coercive of which are mere delusions of the undestined.

"JACK SMITH," I shouted into the phone. "His name is Jack Smith! Not Jacques Smeeze!"

Oui oui, that was him, Jacques Smiss. It was le docteur Ravassard. Monsieur Smiss was in intensive care, he had been the unfortunate victim of a terrorist attack, had lost a leg, he was in his third day of coma, there was concern that he might not, he might not, there was a piece of paper in his wallet with my name and coordinates, le docteur Ravassard knew nothing, of course, of my rapports with Monsieur Smeeze, Monsieur Smiss that is, nothing at all, but one must, under the circumstances, try everything, cut oneself in four, shake sky and earth.

I remember very well the moment I woke up. One of the feathery, owlish moments of my life. I woke up in an unknown, curtained bed, in an unknown room, buried under pounds of unknown, white, watchful eyes.

I thought I was dead. Truly. I thought I had died and gone to heaven. Silly. But that is precisely what I thought.

And Manon, who was there, Manon was a spirit, an angel of a very high order, a principality.

I sat in my corner of the hospital room and I trembled. Machines gurgled and blinked at me as they nourished my man Jack. The occasional nurse came and went. Hours came and went.

Until le docteur Ravassard entered and, observing his machines, said to me:

"Vous êtes, vous avez été, l'amante de M. Smiss?"

His lover? No no. Mr. Smith just stood in front of me once. He had been waiting for two days. He was sour-smelling. He fell asleep in a floral sofa in a hotel. He never called me after that.

But that is not what I said. I said:

"Oui."

The electroencephalograph, according to le Docteur Ravassard, indicated increased activity. He was intrigued, excited. He wanted very much to see if Jack would respond to sexual stimulus. It might very well, he felt sure, push him towards the surface. Of course, any medical technician could, in principle, perform the stimulation. But how much better if it were done, the stimulation, with complicity, if Mr.

Smiss were to recognize . . . le chuchotement de la main . . . the whispering of the hand . . .

And so, as le docteur Ravassard monitored Jack's brain, I slid my whispering hand under the covers, and touched, caressed, the mere sleeping surface of his fair, his Canadian sex.

"No," said le docteur after a time, "No, I do not believe there is response."

He turned from his machine then and looked at me.

"And you," he said. "You are crying. This means there is no response, or this means there is?"

He smiled. An inscrutable, oily smile. A sob surged from my throat like a piece of broken, frothy glass. I pulled my hand away quickly and stuffed it under my arm, not knowing whether, not knowing to this day whether, it was simply one of le docteur's snide amusements.

Nevertheless, Jack woke up a few hours later.

And that is how we met.

My artificial leg works remarkably well. It is Canadian too, by the way. Not subject to corrosion or disease. I am very comfortable with it. It has become my belaying pin, my alias.

I was not happy about it, of course, at first. But at no time have I been in great pain. Pain, yes. Certainly. I have suffered, but not . . . at no time have I ever thought I might prefer the great bland beyond.

I have been, or rather my leg has been, the eye in a bitter hurricane of wrangling over costs and compensation. It could be argued that my accident has represented for me a rather comfy investment. I am not necessarily happy about that either.

Manon has been my principal advocate. Unplacable. She is ferocious when her teeth are bared.

She, for one, will not accept that destiny is, by definition, clandestine.

The Italians, you see, doubting, no doubt quite rightly, of their ability to resuscitate Jack, and afraid he might die on their soil, had flown him, coma and all, back to Lyon.

The Italian authorities seemed to think that people who gave concerts in buildings built by Italian industrialists who also sold sheet metal at enormous personal gain to Libyan interests, sheet metal which was purportedly then resold to the Saudi-Shiite-Syrian-Emirates and used to construct barracks to house the throngs of hapless faithful who quote volunteered unquote to take part in all manner of gruesome, flesh-curdling experiments, that such people should expect terrorists to stick bombs in their French horns. Imagine getting up on the stage like that without taking the simple precaution of putting on a fire-proof body suit.

Eight years later, eight, they awarded Jack x number of million liras. He went out and bought a hat with the money, if I'm not mistaken.

He had an animal's courage. He did not paddle among the lily-pads of anxiety, self-sorrow, guilt-edged pity, and all the usual, leaky, human miserabilities. He stood up like a fallen elk, and he walked. He learned to control, to animate his prosthesis, rather than let it deaden him.

We were, we have been, inseparable. I have coddled him,

cajoled him, cudgeled him. I have held him up until my head was spinning from the pain in my shoulders. And I have kicked his cane away and made him go on alone. He has screamed at me, and I have screamed right back. He has hit me as hard as he could, and I have hit him as hard as I could. And we have fallen asleep together, fully-clothed, on the floor, by the stairs, exhausted. We were inseparable.

I got away from Manon every chance I could. It was not hard. She could never smell the lies on my breath.

She was not satisfied, of course, that I could walk. I had to walk naturally, so that no one would know, so that when people found out they would be astonished. She said that often: you're going to astonish people.

Oh I know. I realize I do walk well. Astonishingly well.

But if she could manage to overcome my plucklessness, why could she not cure me of my relentless craving to love and be loved? My need, as Saint A. puts it, to roll in the cinnamon-scented mud? Eh? Why? Why could she not?

Pick a name at random:

Cherokee. I never knew her by any other name.

5, rue Berçot

78-82-46

Long, Aberdeen-Angus-black pigtails, spaced teeth, unnatural, inventive eyes, like wet stones. I was Lieutenant Rip Rivers. Reep Reevairse. She talked to me in baby-French, the way the Indian squaws talk in dubbed American westerns. She would find me on the open plain, delirious, trampled by wild horses, would drag me to a sheltered place, her buckskin fringes falling in my face, nuzzle me, nurse me, make me eat roasted cowbirds (quails), and dried buffalo meat (Morteau sausage), tear her chemise into strips to rub my stump with cactus milk (plain yogourt), and paint me with spittle and blood (spittle and blood).

Each time I left Cherokee and our elaborate pastimes, the afternoon sun ground itself into my depleted eyes.

Why could Manon not pull the fish-hook, poisoned with candy, out of my palate, the chocolate gaff out of my heavying flesh?

He always kept busy. Always found work. He was wonderful with young people, gave music lessons to all the children in the neighbourhood.

And then, one day, he came home very morose, stinking, *stinking* of Morteau sausage, and said he had to go back to Canada.

And so we did. It seemed as evident as day following night. I should have expected it. I should have thought of it myself.

It was all quite easy. Five months later, we were buying our groceries at Sobey's, in Halifax.

Ah Canada. That pays translators, such as I, such miraculous amounts of money.

Jack went to the Stella Maris one day. The seaman's house. He met the chaplain, who took an interest in him and gave him maintenance work to do. They became fast friends. It's the chaplain who calls him "my man Jack."

One day, I found them in the chaplain's office. Jack was picking through the chaplain's hair. They looked like a pair of chimpanzees.

"What on earth are you men doing?" I said.

"Oh," said the chaplain, "I made the mistake of saying to your man Jack that only God knows the number of hairs growing on my head. Matthew, chapter 10, verse 30. He's counting them now."

"This little tuft," said Jack, "contains 327 hairs. About. Now then, what's the formula for the surface of a sphere?" They finished with an estimate of over 350,000, by the way.

"Imagine," said Jack, "if you had only one hair and it grew, by itself, as much as all of them combined. It would drag from here to Texas."

He was glowing of course. They both were.

Yes, but I spend so much time now searching the one scenario for my history's life. For all my tucking Saint Augustine under my vest, my every conviction dries with time into a brittle diversion. I don't seem to know how to look like I look, how to juggle with the art of the fugitive. I see Manon in my mirror, and my face cracks. From here to here. I miss her. I have missed her so much, my aim is blurred. I just blink and blink, and miss her again.

Where are we? Older, older. Halifax. Manon is translating. I'm repainting the seaman's house for, with, the chaplain. My sheets and hair are spotted with antickity blue.

We had an old metal garbage can which Manon wanted to throw away. She put it out with the other clamjamfry, but the garbage men, of course, left it behind. She put it out the following week, and again, after the truck passed, the can was still there. She phoned the city, she was starting to froth at the mouth, I was enjoying it all, she lay in wait for the garbage collectors, but they went careering by in a flash of clattering dust and she didn't have time to tell them to take the can, she was in a foul mood for a week, she waited for them again, this time at the bottom *of the stairs, and still she missed them, she ran outside, picked the garbage can up and started running with it, shouting, she stumbled and fell, and barked and banged, and ended in a heap.*

Her back was so still, I knew she was crying.

"C'mon," I said, fraternal. "Did you hurt yourself?"

She stayed stuck to her can.

"Viens-t'en. Tout de suite!" Dictatorial.

"Ive lmp," she sobbed.

"What?"

"I have a lump."

"That's too bad. Show me where."

She looked at me then, her face melting under her tears.

"In my troat," she said, pointing at her neck.

"In your throat?"

She nodded. And then she shook her head.

"No, not in my throat. Here!" she sobbed, pressing her arm against her chest. "I have breast cancer."

Jack is right. Destiny's eyes are made of stone.

I am no longer me. It is horrible, horrible, horrible. I have done all this so badly. I cannot get a hold of myself. I am a creeping lachrymosity, my head is full of sausage, my heart full of worms. I'm losing my breast, my coconut, my néné, I shall be jug-ectomized, December 12. *Whop*, catch it nurse, it's a slippery guy, to be chucked, flurp, like a beached jelly-fish, into the waste basket full to bursting with squeaking dugs.

You see? I wallow. It's so easy, so sad I can't stop.

And my man Jack who has no moods, who was, in any case, born seventeen hundred years too late, who quotes from Saint Augustine's *De Musica* to counter the chaplain who cites him back the letter of Paul to the Houyhnhnms, the two painting on together, my man Jack who belabours my humiliatingly clever cowardice by the very facts of his life and his unbearable determination, thank God for my man Jack.

I don't know what to do for Manon. I stay away. I'm not proud of myself.

I should know what she's going through, but I don't. I'm the man who got his leg blown off by terrorists.

Did you really?

I bend my knee by tightening my buttock.

Do you really?

It is not simply that my leg has become a part of my body. My body has become a part of my leg. I'm fine. I'm a lop-sided, gimpy conversation piece.

It has nothing whatever to do with fortitude. Your destiny stops being your destiny when it starts happening to you.

Then it's just a distraction. Something to do.

Did you hear that, Saint A.? Not bad, eh, Saint A?

What do you mean you like Manon's better?

It is not for myself. I am too ancient now to care about myself for myself. I could, if need be, turn into one of the thousands of semi-monthly-permanented, perma-minty ladies, with a drawerful of hypoallergenic bra stuffers, raspberry-peach for Mondays, vanilla-pear for Tuesdays, and who would know except me, and I can learn to keep my dissimulations to myself. Or I could flaunt it, and join committees and breast-cancer-research-lobby-groups and God knows that would be praisewhile and worthworthy. Or I could even parade around in a one-cupper for all the world . . .

But Jack. Jack is a perfectionist. He must have things his way.

Every tick of the clock brings me a second closer to the moment.

Over and over I see myself, from behind, from the side, from above, I see the dress, the slip, the bathrobe, made of mohair, of leather, of 80% cotton, 20% dacron, of summer silk, slide slide slide from my shoulders. Every second I see it, over and over and over. Every second brings me closer to the moment when I must, because it will have to be me, Jack will be too considerate, too discreet to do it, when I will have to unbutton every button.

My brain goes black. I have a splinter in my eye, a nail in my throat. I must unbutton. We all must. And Jack, with his unbearable strength, will manage the tenderest of tender smiles.

And look at my ears.

I think of Manon's breasts as they were, exhausted, falling to each side, falling asleep, the spent nipples closing, drying, beached by the retreating storm of saliva and sweat.

I remember how, long ago in the hospital in Lyon, she so discreetly arranged herself on top of me, with such breathless precaution and with such open desire, that my heart cracked and I looked away.

I looked away. How long have I been looking away?

I think of Manon's new, her twentieth-century chest, and I am filled with that suffocating, hot curiosity that I have not known since I was a boy and my younger sister asked me, in her cunning way, if I thought it was possible for girls to have moles on their nipples. I see my hand moving over Manon's breastplate, I imagine the tingling in my nose as I secretly smell, the taste of her fresh-grown skin on my lips.

Don't stare, Jack, she will say, uneasy, wanting to cry.

I am mesmerized, I cannot help it, I see the one blind, aging nipple groping for its partner, I see the new boyish sternum off and running on its own.

I think: this and any body's beauty, as I see it, lies in the wounds it heals well.

So let us climb into bed together. The three of us. Not that we have children. No. No. But we are a family of three all the same.

So let the three of us climb into bed. I, with my well-turned rig for a leg, Manon with her elegant scar for a breast, and, lying stiffly between us, our shivering, pudgy, well-intentioned destiny, which, as Manon says, has two pieces of coal for eyes. A carrot for a nose.

THE PREMIER'S NEW PYJAMAS

I was dreaming about a man wearing boxing gloves as red and thick as kidneys.

That is to say, I was writing a speech for the premier about a boxer who was being inducted into the Missouri Sports Hall of Fame. An excellent American who, as it happened, was not only born in one of Canada's ten provinces, but had even lived the first three years of his life there.

The premier of the province in question was, therefore, invited to St. Louis to attend the induction dinner and, of course, to say a few hundred words.

Which I, the premier's speech writer, was in the process of preparing.

It was not yet seven in the morning. I had been working for some time. I started before five, usually, writing myself hoarse even before the daily tide of press releases, letters, toasts and endorsements submerged the stony beach of my discursive reason.

Each item was a dream. Thirty seconds after writing it, I could not remember a single word. If I remember the dream about the St. Louis boxer's kidney-gloves, it is because I was roused in the middle of writing it by a tintamarre of people stamping and singing their way down the corridor outside my door.

I opened the door. A young woman made a sour face at me as she passed by. She had a sleeping bag draped across her shoulders. They all had sleeping bags, or blankets and pillows, they were all wearing Mountie hats with toy provincial flags poked into the points, they were clacking their thermos bottles, or their foil plates, or their folding garden chairs. I closed the door, turned, and there he was.

The premier.

"I can't be here," he said.

And I, my surprise undermining my generally dependable sense of fawning deference, "How did *you* get in?"

"Ahhhh," he said, a gleam in his voice. And then, "The place is crawling with students. I can't be here. Have you got your car parked downstairs?"

Early 70's, by the way. A meagre time, in my estimation. Deceitful. Inept. The assassinators, after a string of glorious successes, had managed only to disable as motionless a target as George Wallace. And the student movement was still staging sit-ins, still straining drily for attention.

"Yes," I said. "Sir."

"Prepare to leave. I'll be back in a matter of minutes, no more."

He pressed his thumb into the wall then. There was a muted click, and a concealed door opened. He looked at me without the trace of a smile, raised his eyebrows slyly once, and disappeared through the doorway. I found the button he had pressed, the door clicked open. I closed it again. Opened it, stuck my head through into the penumbra where a dim, carpeted staircase descended indolently, and closed the door again, my throat thick already with dreams of sexual encounters.

When the premier reappeared, he was wearing a wig with sideburns, a false moustache, and a pair of black-rimmed glasses with rectangular lenses.

"Ready?" he said. And down the carpeted staircase we went, along a turning, footlit corridor to a heavy door which the premier shouldered open cautiously. The standard-spring-time sunlight ricocheted off the chrome of the cars parked in the lot outside, skimmed past us sideways, and disappeared down the corridor.

"What kind of car do you drive?" he whispered.

"A Sprite."

He nodded knowingly, it not being permitted for the premier to admit ignorance on any topic whatsoever.

"Lead the way," he said. "Don't hurry."

He was a little excited fitting himself into my car, which was very small. He wriggled and huffed. The seat springs cursed under their breath.

"We'll take the Algord Road," he said.

And so we did. The sky was stuffed with several atmospheres of blue. The leaves on the poplars lining the road applauded as we passed. There was adventure in the premier's presence, so close beside me, the thick, vegetable odour of sleep still clinging to the beard he had not shaved.

"Have you had breakfast?" he said.

"Not really, no."

So we stopped to eat, and after the waitress had brought the coffee, the premier pulled a flask out of his jacket pocket. He topped up first mine, then his own cup.

"Ever live in a comic strip before?" he said.

"You mean the moustache and glasses? You don't look so comical."

He raised his eyebrows in doubt.

"If anything you look more like a premier."

"Speech writer," he said, snorting. And then, assuming his disguise extended to me, which perhaps it did, "Have you ever traveled incognito before?"

"Wale now," said I, talking Texas, "ever' day."

I am homosexual. Was, I suppose. McCorkingdale, my constant and best, my prickly companion, my bippy, bowsprit and organ of non-reproduction, McC. stays to himself pretty much now. I ain't gay. I go back far too far. Just good and queer.

Gays are great, but. Gay families like with kids and all? Yikes. I always thought families were horrible things full of perfumed hatred and fragrant jealousy, even when they weren't full of screaming and tears.

I thought, no doubt ingenuously, that gentle men preferred men, that homosexual relationships were, therefore, as fugitive as tenderness, unetched by snarling, or snooping, or teaming up.

I thought that joy, by nature, is more joyous in the closet than parading in the streets. No?

At any rate, I was, in my time, a subversive. Nobody knew me. I cultivated the vocabulary, the humours of men, so I could navigate among them, hail them, listen to the clatter of their winches, the creaking of their hulls. All men. Square, squeamish, dainty or crude, bad-breathing, flaccid or beau. Their handshakes thrilled me, their queer jokes made me laugh and laugh. Me and McC.

Which, out of so many, were, like me, the fairies with their wings tied down? Which were the sleight of heart men? Which? This simple question informed all, all my meetings, jostlings, left me deliciously perplexed, expectant, irrationally so. If I suspected my interlocutor of giving me so much as the ghost of a look, I was stiflingly happy. I shot off immediately a box of many-coloured flares hoping to see at least one reflected in his eye. I seldom did.

Oh, I studied physiognomy hard under every kind of light, and dark, but I never really learned to spot another queer.

I had fairly good ideas, of course.

I had a fairly good idea about the premier.

He ate a little toast with his jam, the premier did. The jam he fed himself by the tablespoonful, directly from the jar. He ordered me another coffee, slipped me his flask, and went off to phone. Twenty minutes later, he came skulking back, tapping his leg with a rolled-up newspaper.

"Ready?" he said.

We walked together to the cash, he looking nervously at the floor, I fumbling for my wallet.

Outside he said, "I don't have any money with me. I don't usually carry any."

"No problem."

"I don't have a driver's license either." And then, reasserting no doubt his exceptional identity, "I do have my will. It's folded in seven and taped to my thigh."

"I'll drive carefully anyway."

And drive we did. The new cornfields, planted as systematically as a doll's scalp, parted for us endlessly. Far back floated the white clusters of buildings that would in another ten weeks be hidden by the deepening crops.

"It is on days like these," said the premier, his false moustache bobbing, "that I most enjoy being the central administrative figure of this province. If I could, I would take every school child for a drive down this road, and many others like it."

"May I point out," said I, "that it is the school children, the university-age children, who are undermining your administrative program. Who do not apparently believe in the defining principles of our society. Or any other society known to man."

"But," said the Premier, "that is what I find so exciting. It is not true to say the students do not accept our society. They want something, yes. But they also think they can get it. Doesn't our society define success as finding a way to get what you want? I like people who want. I want them."

I want them. The words sniffed at McCorkingdale like the shiny nose-leather of a substantial dog. "The students," I said, reddening, "don't know what it is to want. They've gotten too used to getting."

"As you say, children who get make adults who want."

"I said that?"

"Adults though, unlike children, have to keep thinking up things to want to get themselves. Lack of necessity is the father of creativity. Hoo, I've read so many of your speeches, I'm starting to sound like you."

There was, of course, nothing I could say to this.

It is not without bemusement that I report my part in this conversation. I did, in fact, support the students to a considerable extent. Note, however, that the vast majority of my verbal production tumbled into existence through the mouths of others. Always distorted. If not by the speaker's grafting his own lexis onto mine, then by faulty microphones, by the sound of saliva mixing with trout inside the mouths of eating listeners, by the wind. So that I did not often pay attention to the distortions of my voice when it tumbled out of my own mouth. In any case, the premier, by now, was on another tack.

"Myrtleville," he said. "A remarkable town. The deciduous tree line cuts right through here. You can see it perfectly from the air, poplar and aspen on the south, conifers on the north. Look! Some of the white pines are four hundred years old. We should pay a visit to Alfie Gallant. His farm is off Markham Road, just past the creamery."

Alfie Gallant. Unbeatable. Every January, a hundred or so short-headed snowshoers raced headlong some thirty-three miles up the frozen Massapatawquish River to a clearing, built a fire there only large enough to make tea and raced right back again. Frostbite was part of the fun. And Alfie Gallant was unbeatable.

"Every year," said the premier, "as I stand at the finish line, I'm afraid Alfie will win again. I think to myself this will be the year when, at last, he'll turn into the braggart. And every year he manages to contain his barn-sized ego inside his half-way smile. His farmer's smile. When the rain falls, at last."

I was flattered that he was talking to me in this way, not as speech writer, but as apprentice say, conveying to me the nature of his province, the province of his own government-high ego.

"And every year," he said, "I'm afraid Alfie will not be first."

On and on we drove, the premier dozing, knees wedged against the dashboard, head tilted back, glasses over his forehead.

"When I was a student," he muttered, "I didn't have the slightest idea what I wanted to do. I knew a lot of things I didn't want to do, so I eliminated all those. The list got longer and longer, until all that was left was premier. You?"

You? The question licked at me hesitantly, seeking encouragement.

"Me?" I said. "Oh, I eliminated premier right off the bat."

And he, yawning, "Wise man."

"Are you going to sleep now?"

"Might."

"Do you want me just to keep driving then till we get to Paraguay?"

"You can if you like. Or you can stop at Eleanor's."

"Eleanor's is a restaurant somewhere? A motel?"

"No, Eleanor is my mother. Eleanor's is where she lives."

"My, my, my," she said, "what are *you* doing here?"

She was a short woman, Eleanor was, humourously short beside her tall son. The undercurl of her dry hair brushed her shoulders when she turned her head. Her skin was grainy from long hours spent not so much in the sun, as in the open. She wore a shirtwaist dress, the lowest buttons left undone to reveal her legs, sturdy and balanced, the strong calves curved like overturned dinghies.

Striking legs. McCorkingdale, self-willed as ever, craned to catch a glimpse.

"A horde of university students," said the premier, "are crawling over my desk at this very moment. Haven't you heard?"

"Yes." Her voice was as husky as her skin. "I also heard somewhere that you were the central administrative figure of this province and that your place was, therefore, in the capital city. I may have misheard."

"You may have. I am, in fact, the premier."

"Ah," pausing, looking directly into his eyes. "And this gentleman is . . .?"

"Mr. Watson. No, no. Mr. Gilfillan. What was I thinking of to make me say Watson? Mr. Gilfillan. My speech writer."

"Aaaahhhh. You'll be able to deliver a speech in the kitchen then."

"Or the greenhouse, or the lava-tree, wherever. The bedroom if you like."

"I think I may have had enough bedroom speeches for one lifetime. Unless. Are you particularly good at bedroom speeches Mr. Wa . . .?"

"Gilfillan," said the premier quickly.

"I'm sorry. Mr. Gilfillan. Mr. Gilfillan looks like he has

been driving a car for several hours and would like something to eat. Come." She hooked her arm into mine. "Tell me how it is you manage to make my son sound as though he had learned something at school, and not simply studied law."

Watson. What was he thinking of to make him say Watson? Oh I knew, I knew. The sly puss-'n-boots. I trembled with the familiar ebullience. The frothy darkness pushed itself into my eyes, I could hear my hand knock once and once only, could feel them all breathing.

"My son, you see," went on Eleanor, leading us into a well-appointed kitchen with a thickset, not to say corpulent, wooden table, blazing with varnish, "my son is of the old school, the old King Cole school. He believes political leaders should give the impression that good God himself inflated their little lungs at birth, licked his thumb and touched it to their forehead. That they should be dignified, up-beat, meat pie with gravy? Be alright? Conniving, bursting with probity and hot air, and entirely without talent. Or children. Surely a man in such a position could arrange to have children. A daughter-in-law I don't require. But children, grandchildren."

Watson's. My dear Watson's. Although it may have been a slip. He did not, perhaps, know about Watson's.

"He does not," she went on, "seem to be aware," no, he knew, he did, he was sitting on the table now eating olives, "that while he doubtless makes a rare prime rib of a minister, dolled up in his shimmering eye-talian civvies," holding the pits in his hand, My Dear Watson's, where you went down to the mens' room, the oven door clanging shut, "it does not last forever, his body is increasingly ovoid, his nose is getting puffier and puffier with long drinks and circumlocution," the premier squeezing his nose to see if it were swollen, his good humour attenuated with consternation, "one must eventually *do* something with one's life, musn't one? What point is there in history scratching its head to remember a name that no one else does, except me, and who is to remember me, except he?"

The gravy caramelizing on the stove, Eleanor's pebbly voice glinting across the table, and I, I was dreaming about Watson's, an Englishy pub with leatherette seats, pictures of London in the rain at night, waiters in Sherlock Holmes hats. My Dear Watson's, to the heavy-smelling blackguards of queerdom. Down you went to the men's room. You did not go in, mind you, you went past it to the next door, your hand trembling as you knocked lightly once and once only, the door no sooner open than the darkness behind it sucked you inside. You could see nothing but you could hear the humid, lupine breathing of a dozen men, not a word, not a word, but the pulse in your neck like a trapped insect, you were taken hold of then, you were hoisted over the heads of the dozen men, you floated on their quick, unhurried, invading hands pulling your clothes away. You dipped and rolled, but they would not put you down, you shuddered and arced on their palping, kissing hands, you were drowning in your own, you were awful, awful, and they would not put you down. You merely woke up alone, if you were me, in your corner, ill with exhaustion, naked, sticky, your underwear still stopping your mouth, your genitals aching, until someone knocked lightly once and once only, the door opened wide enough only for a hand to reach in and turn on the lights.

"Goodness, Mr. Gilfillan," said Eleanor, "do you always eat like three horses?"

You were in a storeroom, there were huge jars of mustard, of instant gravy powder, tubs of shortening, a bundle of clothes smelling of fabric softener was thrown in to you quickly, and the door was closed.

"And are you always as quiet as a carp?"

Is there, thought I, any way to shut this woman up?

"Well now," said the premier, "the students, like everyone else in the province, think I'm on my way to St. Louis, and to get me to come back quick, they will have to all go quietly home. Of this they have been made abundantly aware. Now as I see it, the boy students will not sleep tonight for agonizing over the accessability of the sweet bodies breathing beside them, the girls will not sleep for being constantly on the alert to yank the boys' hands out of their sleeping bags. There will be those, of course, very likely a plurality, who will not sleep for finding the parliament building too exotic a location to resist. They will all, tomorrow, be tired and testy and faced with the cold thought that fun is fun, but to get what they want they need me."

"Premiers," said Eleanor, "like to feel needed."

"I think," said the premier, "one night should do it. Two at the most. Feel like staying a night or two, Derek?"

Derek was me.

"I'm sure," said Eleanor, "Mr. Gilfillan has better things to do with his days. Has he clothes with him? Pyjamas?"

"I bought half a dozen pairs of new pyjamas the last time I was here," said the premier. "I haven't even opened half of them. I'll put a box on the bed. So."

He finished his coffee standing up, waved, and was gone.

There was a moment, a band of silence. And then Eleanor swept her arm across the table in front of her, bowl and plate, utensils, glass and place mat all sent soaring, rushing up to the ceiling where they floated and circled with the unbearable slowness of ships in a sea port seen from the air. Until the tears welling up in her lower lids compelled her at last to blink, and down crashed the dishes onto the red-tiled floor, the place mat gliding obliquely into the sink.

"Shhhh!" she hissed at me fiercely. "Listen. You can still hear his footsteps climbing the stairs."

I confess I could not. I can not fathom the ability of women to hear the faintest sounds in their houses. She sputtered and fustigated, my astonished ears heard the word "faggot" squeak out of the side of her mouth like a breathy note from a cold flute. She took, from out of the cupboard under the sink, a dustpan and whisk.

"Let me do that for you," I said, getting up smartly.

"Over my dead body!" she snapped.

I do not remember the bedroom well. There were a lot of wooden things, there were magazines and Chivas. The bedspread I do remember. It was as green as green, and served as a field for the sleek black and gold box lying on it casually.

I drank and waited. The intense, country silence clung to me, moved when I moved. I waited. And drank.

Until I could no longer put it off. Undress I must. Open the box I must, I must. Open the box I did.

The black and gold box, which was empty.

The sly puss-'n-boots.

I lay in the dark, dressed only in the premier's new pyjamas, shivering between the glossy sheets, awaiting his majesty's silk-draped flesh to enter by some secret door and have at me, I was twisting with sex, I was tired, tired, I had driven too far, I had eaten too much, the whiskey was turning to acid in my intestines, and Eleanor insisted on dancing over me. Eleanor, dancing over my dead body, her shirtwaist dress knifing through the night so close to my face, snicking at my nose, her stoney legs opening in silence, opening to reveal the crown of his-majesty-to-be. I lay shaking between the sheet-metal sheets, I wanted to sleep, only to sleep, but the premier was coming, and I could not stop crying.

The door opened. The tiger lept.

McCorkingdale stood hard to attention.

In poked a head.

Enter, enter, murmured McCorkingdale. Bring on the body politic.

But it was not the premier.

"Sleep well?" said Eleanor.

"Sleep? What time is it?" said I, instantly awake, rolling onto my side to hide McC.

"Ten past seven. Did you find the pyjamas?"

"Ahh, yes."

She sat on the edge of the bed, sending a ripple through the mattress that made McC. tingle. She looked vaguely in the direction of the window.

"He left during the night," she said.

"Who did?"

"He did. With his cabinet chief and the minister of transports of delight."

"Pardon me?"

"His pals."

"Oh. When did all this take place?"

"Two-thirty. Three."

"I didn't hear anything," I said, piqued, foolishly.

She turned towards me then.

"You're a very good speech writer, Mr. Derek Gilfillan." She placed her palm on the bed beside me. McCorkingdale, fascinated, strained towards her.

I thought, for a moment, that it was snowing in the bedroom.

"Goodness," she said. But it was not snow that was falling. She had a freckle on her colourless lip. It was dust perhaps. Particles of dust swollen with light, it may have been that.

"You are not very substantial for a man who eats like three horses." Sequins or spangles or tiny Venetian coins.

"He's a bit of a murderer in his way," she said. "I know." Venetian chocolate coins tossed into the sunlight from the Rialto bridge. "We have only one life," she said, "but one life that is wrapped in so many existences. It's good to get murdered every now and then, to kill off an outer existence or two. They get dry and papery and peel away, and then we are a little closer at least to our life. Of course we are also white and juicy and ready for more murder." Or words, palatal glides and fricatives for all I know, or seeds perhaps, dandelions. "Nothing murders like not being loved very much. But then, when you are not loved, you are not anyone. So you can become . . . anyone. Every big ambition begins with a small murder." Or meteorites, quite possibly meteorites, but they were not actually falling. "Look at all these bourgeois silverfish who sleep with their windows locked and never dare try manslaughter unless it is brought to them by Kellogg's. Bfff." It was the light slowly turning that made them appear to fall. "Look at them with their precious existences interlarded with bulletproof foam. Bfff." A parti-coloured particular ray shot occasionally into my eye. "You are not one of them, Derek." They were floating, they must have been, because they did not accumulate on the floor, it was the light slowly turning, it was the light that accumulated. "The three horses you eat like have wings," said Eleanor, her hand on my knee, her palping, kissing words washing like smoke over McCorkingdale, turning the particulate air into solid light, I could not see for it all, I could not breath, I was awful, awful, is there not, I pleaded, *any* way to shut this woman up.

So we got out of bed we did. McCorkingdale and I.

"Mmn," said Eleanor, "Very nice. The pj's. Just your colour."

"Eleanor," I said, dressing, "you're very good at speeches. Very. I write his. That's all. Sometimes he even reads them. I do his press releases. I answer his letters, of which, by the way, an astonishing number are from women, of a confessional nature, often intimate, usually intelligent. I enjoy it. I forget everything thirty seconds afterwards. Everything."

I drove back then, and as I did so, I heard over and over Eleanor's words, felt McCorkingdale rise towards her husky voice.

And when I arrived, there were squads of cleaners in the otherwise empty corridors. I slid my key into the knob of my office door, but before I had time to turn it, the door was opened from the inside.

"You made good time," whispered the premier. He slid one of his prestigious buttocks onto the edge of my desk, drank coffee, high-octane presumably, from a paper cup. Anita Devlin, the student leader, quite high-octane herself with her hair as straight as water and her mouth full of braces, was reading intently in my chair.

"You knew I was on my way?"

"Eleanor phoned to say you were coming. She keeps tabs on us all." He leaned toward me. "She called the papers," he murmured, strong with coffee and cologne, "in the middle of the night. Pretended to be one of the neighbours. Said I'd been seen at her house."

"Are you sure?"

"Of course. She told me. We'd have been better off staying at Alfie Gallant's, eh? You are to come any time, by the way, and not wait for me to invite you."

"Miss Devlin!" he said then. Miss Devlin looked up, high matters in her eyes, entirely, I would say, under the premier's power. "I'd like you to meet my speech writer, Derek Gilfillan. Hot awful good on his good days. Look at this. It's the dinner speech I was to give tonight in St. Louis."

"What are the drawings in the margin?" said Miss D. "They look like kidneys."

"Kidneys?" said I.

"Now that you're here, Derek," said the premier, "we'll give you your office back."

He pressed his thumb into the wall then, there was a muted click, and the concealed door opened.

"Oohh," said Miss D., duly sarcastic, duly impressed, "secret passages and all."

The premier guided her past him into the dim, carpeted penumbra.

"Eh!" he said suddenly.

"What's up?" said I.

"The pyjamas."

"The pyjamas?"

"I was going to leave a box of new pyjamas on the bed for you, wasn't I?"

"You did."

"I did?"

"There was a box."

"There was. Eleanor must have put it there for you then. Good for her. What *would* we do without Eleanor." He looked at me without the trace of a smile, raised his eyebrows slyly once, and disappeared through the doorway.

Jilted I was. Murdered. Just as Eleanor said. Jilted, jealous. But in love, in love.

"Faggot!" I squeaked out of the side of my mouth, to prove it. McC. was feeling forgotten. Weren't you, McC.? But what do you know about love?

"*Fa*ggot!" Joyously.

A one-word speech, of course. A curt dream.

THE BREEZE BEING NEEDED

My father was, is, an ambulance driver in Saint Catharine's, Ontario, of Egyptian distraction, whose name was, *is*, Ossama Bashur (as is mine). He has been attempting for years to melt into the developed-occidental decor – 12-handicap Lion's Clubber, campaign chairman for the vice-mayor – has been melting, therefore, like a red ice-cube into clear water. Because he *is* Egyptian, and was so even in 1947 when he arrived with his little post-war English tradesman's certificate and his stoutly Canadian wife (hi Mom). He has had, consequently, certain things happen to him – all part of the normal residue of human nature churning out its obtuse and self-congratulatory destiny – but certain things all the same, and as a result of these certain things, I was shipped off when I was three to the city of Madison to stay with my mother's elder brother and his Wisconsin wife where at least there was food.

I had a vision in Madison.

A sinewy woman was my Aunt J., with a wilted face, as though the pressure inside her head had dropped for an instant below atmospheric pressure, very strong and with acidulous breath, which led me to think she ate flowers. Moved by a sense of disciplined commiseration with her sister-in-law, she never let me forget that my true home was not Madison. "You're a Canadian, Ozzie," she would say to me. But I was still in a pre-geographic phase of life, my only nation was my bed, everything else a foreign territory where I might at any time and for no apparent reason be asked to report on the nature of my activities. I had at best the ghost of an idea what the word meant, the word "Canadian" that is, so that each time it was spoken it spread over my tingling brain like magic smoke, its billowy, white sound screening me from the fluttering dove of its true definition.

I say vision. A vision is generally held to be a hot and blasty affair associated with many fathoms of light. Not mine.

Although I did have one important clue as to what a Canadian, like I was, was. The clue was not contained in my memory, which was still something of a toy, an album of moments I played with only occasionally. Nor was it contained in the geo-political catechism to which my aunt regularly submitted me: "North America is a continent, Ozzie, divided into two countries, the United States of America and . . . Ca? . . . Can? . . . Oh Ozzie! Kansas City's a city!" The clue was contained rather in the figure of a man of contradictory characteristics. He was tall and trim in his good clothes, gawky in shorts. His great-smile occupied so much of his face that it pushed his cheeks out of the way into his eyes which dropped out of sight completely. It was, to me, an analgesic smile that revealed, nevertheless, a mouthful of teeth so large and overlapping that they appeared to grind against each other painfully. He was my Uncle T., and the man to whom my Aunt J. referred when she said to me, "you're just like your uncle, Ozzie, he's a Canadian too, you know, your mother's brother, you haven't got any brothers, or nephews either for that matter, not yet, no."

No, my vision occurred in the chilly semi-darkness of the second story of Aunt J.'s duplex, as, weaving sleepily from my nationroom to the john, I passed in front of their imperfectly closed bedroom door. Aunt J. was not in my field of vision. Uncle T., on the other hand, was. From head to foot. Although it was not either to his head or to his foot that my attention was drawn, but, as was his own attention, to his sex. To its exotic pendulousness, yes. To its leonine hirsutitude, certainly. But above all to its colour. Uncle T. had a little bottle of paint in one hand, an artist's paintbrush in the other. And he was painting himself bright red.

A minim of my imagination was cauterized for ever and good. Even though the bedroom door was firmly closed when I returned from the john, and every time thereafter I attempted to confirm my initial observations, I could expect to review at any moment, willy nilly, the dark hairs running down out of Uncle T.'s navel and all but drowning his crimson, flamboyant mensware. I mused upon my vision at length, mentioning it to no one. It excited me when I was excited, and calmed me when I was calm. It drew me relentlessly into my uncle's intimacy, its glowing secrecy surrounding me, pushing me towards him whenever we were in the same room.

"What's got into you?" he would say, fending me off, and I, with my five-year-old, unmannered intuition, I knew that he was right to do so, that there was something false in my affection, something missing, it was not simply Uncle T. but both of us, me watching Uncle T., that was what I had really seen. I lay in my bed perspiring, seeing myself over and over in my own vision. Until finally it collapsed, the vision did. It turned liquid and drained into all the interstices of my understanding. I knew. I knew why it had been given to me, to *me*, to see Uncle T. Because we were Canadians. The only two for miles and miles. And a Canadian was a man, when he got to be a man, who painted himself red.

After that, I won all the 50-yard dashes and all the spelling bees, and only talked to Uncle T. to ask him to pass the macaroni please, sir. And when my Aunt J. said, "You're *just* like your uncle," I answered, because I so hoped she was right, "I am *not*."

I started Grade 3 in Madison, but I finished it in Saint Catharine's, the circumstances leading to my repatriation being as follows:

My father, having just returned from Quebec where he had gone with a group of local itinerants to pick apples, was in a tavern with the said itinerants when, encouraged by the accumulation of empty glasses on the table, he decided to tell a joke. He would never say what the joke was. As the punch line approached, he could not prevent himself from becoming excited, or his Egyptian-trained vocal apparatus from becoming clogged, with the result that he found himself giggling nervously at the joke he was not managing to put across, hoping to dislodge a little mirth from his confused listeners. His tense hilarity transforming itself into a drunken tantrum, he stomped out of the tavern, was struck by a car and, shortly thereafter, loaded into an ambulance where he regained consciousness in time to see the driver, a pink-faced individual with white eyelashes, slump dreamily over the steering wheel. The driver's partner managed to bring the ambulance to a halt and immediately began massaging the driver's failing heart, while my father, essentially unhurt and instantly sober, jumped behind the wheel and lit out for the hospital all-sirens-ahead. No sooner had they got there than another call came in, another and another, so that when at last he stumbled homeward that morning he was drunk and giggling all over again, the driver having died in the night, and he, my father, having been hired without further ceremony to replace him.

Steady. Money.

This story my father has recounted any number of times, as recently as yesterday, but not, as I believe he should, to satirize the fruit-belt fraternity which instead of silently giving him a job to do, made him be a pledge and rushed him for years, eventually submitting him to an initiation rite worth a photograph and half a surprised page in the local newspaper, a rite whose donalduckleness distracted from its essential shame. No, he recounts the story because he is proud of it and because he likes to reaffirm his adolescent, pledgling admiration for the ambulance driver who gave his life that he, my father, might become a normalized citizen.

In any event, his first act in his new role was to recall definitively his banished son.

I shook my father's hand very dutifully, recognized my own wiry black hair in his, understood why my oddball name was the same as his name, felt his mysteriousness turning the air in my lungs to glass, all the while doing my utmost to silence the alarums drumming in my ears, to frap my cracking self, to stifle the name of Uncle T. swelling longingly in my throat.

Certainty is a stern quality, without nuance or play, domineering, desperate, appealing, strangely, to those who believe themselves least susceptible to desperateness and domination.

And I was as certain as the Sahara is certain: this man, my father, was not a man who painted himself red. Not a Canadian. I would not have it. He was a foreigner.

And here we are, half a lifetime later.

"I have a story for you, Ozzie II."

Stories, he calls them. Jokes they are, just jokes. Millions of the unfunny things, kid's stuff and worse, all meticulously written out on file cards to be taken out during quiet stretches and run through, never to blow another one, the build-ups elaborated and adapted to perfectly suit his rolling butter-cream-eyed style and sing-song voice, the punch lines barely more than cues to his listeners to snort once shortly and ask for another. And I, during much of the same half-lifetime, bouncing from half-success to qualified failure, no sooner engaged as second sax in the 47th regiment sitting-down band than its funding evaporates and it turns into a bugle corpse, my pockets no emptier than the day I was born, my father out of exasperation putting me in charge of an eight-unit apartment I did not even know he owned, although he had 46 other units in various locations and part of a trailer park, and before I knew it I was Mr. Jacob P. Landlord making a chocolate mint housing two-thirds of the half-failures in town.

Of course my vision could not withstand the Canadian climate, the minim of my imagination remained cauterized but a minim is not very much, my certainty soon crumbled, I came to realize that if Uncle T. painted himself red that was his business, my exaggerated fondness for him broke apart into chunks of ribald hilarity, disintegrating further into chips of curiosity, still further into nothing at all, I forgot about the red paint, Uncle T. and Aunt J. too for that matter, not having seen them since even before they separated for lack of children. But if I let my vision sink into the sea with a hiss, I did not therefore grant my father – it being a further characteristic of certainty that the misapprehensions it nourishes continue to grow nicely even though the certainty itself rots away – did not grant him what everyone for miles around was more than happy to grant him, despite his unbearable jokes. Namely, a full and unqualified, a model citizenship.

Toastmaster, realtor, high-sounding politico, ambulance driver, doer, dad. Although ambulance drivers too wind up in hospital beds.

"I grant you," says he, "I have devoted a great deal of energy into prolonging my life, which is only mildly embarassing. Besides, now that I can consider my life distantly, inquisitively, without anger, without hope, as you might consider a thing, a fan say, spinning in its cage, a three-speed speeding fan, it makes a little breeze, good for it, it will do so for as long as a breeze is required and then it will not be a fan any more, so now that I can, now that each day begins with its puff of surprise, by chance, pure chance, Ozzie, we are not responsible for the breeze being needed. Baa, if I put so much effort into being a good shit it is because nothing lasts like good shit. Nobody throws it away because it's good, nobody eats it because it's shit. It just sits there and stinks less and less. Embarassing I grant you, but only mildly. I have a story for you, I got it from the orderly: Two men in a boat. Cigarette? says one. Sure, says the other. Got any matches? says the one. No, says the other. Me neither, says the one. So he fishes another cigarette out of the pack and throws it in the water. Know why?"

"Why," say I.

"So the boat would be a cigarette lighter. Don't laugh."

"I'm not going to laugh," say I.

"Where's the attlebaxe?" says he, the attlebaxe being my mother.

"She's coming," say I.

"Cultivate, Ozzie II, a sense of belonging, and they'll all stop noticing that you don't belong. Ingratiate yourself. Got another story for you, also from the orderly: Mister A: I bought a pair of pants today. Paid way too much. The salesman was from Cairo. Mister B: How do you know he was from Cairo? Mister A: 'e gypt me. Hardy-har. Me and the orderly on the same side at last. See what I mean? Only mildly. Ah, the attlebaxe."

In sashays then my stoutly Canadian, greying mother, high-heels and turquoise rings, necklaces like strings of beaming candies, her flowery dress drifting quietly over the wide plateau of her upper breastwork before falling over the edge and plummeting earthward, my mother, moved by an undemonstrative distrust in all who profess even mild competence in any field whatsoever, together with a cold-eyed, demanding sympathy for the unsuccessful, unlucky, undernourished, underdogged, underloved. In sashays the attlebaxe, delivers greetings: "How are you feeling? How are your movements?" And says, "Tobias and Jean are coming to see you."

Uncle T. and Aunt J., whom I have not seen since even before they were divorced, reunited by Ozzie I's cancer. My heart leaps up.

"Baa," says my father. "Coming to see Ossama you mean."

"Now don't start," says my mother.

What, say I to myself, tension? In connection with Uncle T. and Aunt J.? News to me.

"Don't start what?" say I, lazily.

"Don't *you* start," says my mother.

"What?" say I.

Brief pause for silent, negotiatory calculation.

"Well," says my mother, this being the usual prelude to her conclusive edicts, "your father would just rather not have had to send you to Tobias and Jean's, that's all. Men are proud. Perfectly understandable."

"If you want to know," says my father, unprepared to take the gag, "there was no living with you when you came back. Snarky little six-year-old smartass."

"Yes, well, there's living with him now," says my mother. "That's all that matters surely."

"So damn," says my father, "attached to them. Uncle T. this and Aunt J. that. Your mother found it very difficult."

"Well," says my mother, "in the first place, you underestimate the thickness of my skin. I never minded cutting off the crusts just like Jean did. What you minded was of course just that, that I didn't. In the second place, in the second place, it was Tobias and Jean who got too attached to Ossama."

"Well," says my father, this being the usual prelude to the collapse of his argumentation, "that *might* be true."

"Of course it's true. You gave them their best years, Ossama. You should know that. They did us a great service and they were very devoted to you. So much so, they decided not to have children of their own while you were staying with them. They thought it might be hard for you. And then when you left, the children just didn't come. Terribly sad. Jean sent me letters and letters. It just rankled and festered, and finally they couldn't live with it. Jean was made to have children you know. Tobias too, Tobias too. Terribly sad."

The attlebaxe having chopped a small hole in my heart, I stifle the name of Uncle T. swelling longingly in my throat.

"Sometimes," says my mother, "I think the reason we were never given more children, and we certainly wanted them, was so that Tobias and Jean would not be hurt."

"Oh," says my father, "I thought it was the Mercurochrome."

"God," says my mother, smothering something in the crook of her throat, a guffaw perhaps, a sob, "weren't we stupid though."

"Mercurochrome?" say I.

"You don't need to know about the Mercurochrome, Ossama," says my mother.

"Baa," says my father. "Your Uncle Toby's highly scientific method for not having kids. Paint the appropriate areas with Mercurochrome before getting down to business. Supposed to kill the little tadpoles. Your mother had us doing it for a while. We used other things in conjunction. We weren't completely stupid."

The attlebaxe is trembling. She is laughing silently. She is never so silent as when she laughs.

I had a vision in Madison. A childish misinterpretation of adult ineptitude. Long forgotten in any case. Dropped into the sea with a hiss.

The ambulance driver consolidates his advantage: "Besides, judging by the quality of the business we got down to, birth control was not the only reason your mother wanted us using the Mercurochrome."

The attlebaxe is shaking uncontrollably. It is the way she laughs. Her face is very red, her hair very white. One hand is stopping her mouth, the other is holding her necklaces so they will not rattle. Her eyes are deep in the eyes of the ambulance driver. He is grinning himself, like the White Nile, having flooded the attlebaxe's wide plateau with so much mirth. His prostate gland is blown with cancer. His eyes are deep in the eyes of the attlebaxe. They are both crying.

Tobias and Jean are coming, Uncle T. and Aunt J. having long since split up.

I am the foreigner after all. I have been supplied a passport, yes, but am refused the necessary visa to enter the country of this intimacy.

So I busy myself. Silently. At the edge of the breezeless sea. Pouring sand into the hole in my heart.

THE LACTOSE-INTOLERANT DAUGHTER

I am the lactose-intolerant daughter. I had a raging temper when I was young.

My mother's sweet head, with its creamy curls and cartoon-blue eyes, turned and bobbed alertly atop her squat, inflexible body. She was four-foot-ten. And a quarter. My father, on the other hand, was well over six feet tall. He was, I suppose, a handsome man, in his way, in his harmless way. Bearded, sloppy. Burly in winter; fat in July.

My temper. I might lose it because the peas were hard, or because the button my mother sewed on at the collar of my white blouse was pink.

I had a doll whose eyelids rubbed against the edge of the eye-holes with a dry, grating noise, a slow-witted noise. I would raise and lower this doll time after time so that the eyelids would open and close, and I would hear again and again this sound which was like a hen's claw gradually tearing its way along my spine. Until I was in such an exalted state that anything, my mother's little floating laugh, or the smell of eggs on my father's breath, would cause all the little fires burning along my back to blow into the red hole of a brain that I have, and there would no longer be any doubt, any bravura, any lumps in my existence. There would only be screaming. Screaming, squirming, kicking, and breaking.

My mother would be desperate after these tantrums. Exhausted. My father would have found some reason to leave the house. And I, I would be very soft-eyed, very chalky, and untouchable.

I had a cousin who was five years younger than I was. I did not know her well, she died in a car accident at nineteen. Her husband died with her. I say husband. He was, at any rate, the father of the seventeen-month-old boy who survived them.

I was selling perfumed candles and rattan furniture at the time. My father thought it would be the right thing if I looked after little Nick. For a while.

Sure, I said to myself. Love to. Please, little Nick, eat. Please, little Nick, sleep. Please, little Nick, stop shrieking, your parents will be home in another lifetime.

"We'll help you out with the money side of it," said my father, confidentially, as though we were cooking up a surprise for the late parents, and they musn't find out.

"Oh, the money's okay," I said. Like an idiot.

"You realize, do you, that Nick might be with you . . . for some months."

I can still hear the pearly vagueness of "some months."

How many months did it end up being? Roughly. 250? About that.

He was exasperatingly sweet, was Little Nick. It irritated me that nothing he did irritated me. Long before he learned to talk, he could sing. At fourteen months he was belting out the national anthem, from listening to sports on television.

One day, he came home from grade one, stomped past me through the kitchen, and without even looking up, said, "Hey, good-lookin'."

I was frightened. He was not mine. He could not learn in any orderly way. He could only pick up scraps when and where he wanted, and grind them all into a paste of niceness. He was too simple, too mysterious.

"Nichol P. Henry's the name," he used to say. "Double-draggin's the game."

Because right from the start he was very poor at school. Teacher after teacher, whether bun-haired and auntish, or lanky and concerned, would, at some point in the school year, look me in the face and say, as if they were the first to make the diagnosis, "I'm afraid Nichol has a learning disability." Generally, it was in a gymnasium, there were scattered triangular sandwiches left on paper plates on long wooden tables, there were mothers milling about everywhere, some of them waiting to talk to this same teacher about their wunderkind, not knowing whether to listen in with frank solicitude, or pretend not to hear.

Double-draggin'. I had an old, navy, Raleigh 3-speed. I used to strap little Nick onto the seat, his feet in a pair of stirrups made from belts, and then pedal standing up. Nick called it double-draggin', and we did it for years. Eventually Nick did the pedaling, and I got the seat. We went double-draggin' everywhere, especially on the cemetery hills.

And to a hundred different grocery stores.

It is not difficult, generally speaking, to shoplift from grocery stores. You pay, of course, for bread and milk, a can of condensed soup and so on, and you walk out of the store with your pockets and intimate apparel stuffed to bursting. The truth is, as in any business venture, the more you pay for, the more you can steal.

I've been caught. Many times. So. I break into a sweat, and as always, soon after I start to perspire, I start to cry. I put it all back on the shelves while some needle-toothed woman with skin that cracks like pink icing breathes behind me. So. They distribute your photograph to all the grocery stores in the neighbourhood. You move to a new neighbourhood.

Once, at Christmas, I was just pushing the door open to leave when the hand, barely heavier than its own shadow, placed itself on my shoulder, the voice exploded, pleasantly, "Excuse-me-madam-I-believe-you-dropped-a-glove-back-at-the-cash-if-you'll-just-come-with-me . . ."

There were four of them in the room. "We've been watching you," said one, "for over half an hour." So I started unloading onto the table all the Christmas surprises I had gotten for Nick, the champagne crackers, the olives, the snails, the snail shells, their eyes got rounder and rounder, I kept unloading, capers and smoked salmon and so on, and at the end I pulled out the ice-pack and the frozen duck. One of them got on the phone then, and soon afterward the police officer arrived.

I waited for hour upon hour in the police station. I was hot the whole time. I couldn't keep the perspiration from sprouting at the roots of my hair, or the tears from collecting in my lids, my jaw was aching close to my ears, and I wished I were at the sea, the real sea, grey, noisy, and insolent, where the wind pulls your hair across your mouth, and the sand is cold.

Until a brown-faced man with a horsehair moustache came across me, swore at me, and said, "Do you realize it's two AM in the morning?"

And then he asked me if I was planning to sit there all night long "hiding my light under the bushes," and if I was going to wait all my life for something to happen "like a lump in a bog." And after some more in the same vein, he told me to go with a uniformed woman whose calves were made of shortening.

We went up some stairs and down some stairs and along several corridors, and then she stopped at a cupboard and took down a grey blanket, a grey towel, and some grey powder in a paper cup, which she gave me saying, "The shower's at the far end. Wash. Everywhere."

With one hand she opened a swinging door, and with the other, she guided me through without touching me. I was in a dormitory with tall bare windows through which entered a frosty light, glaucous and wet, so that I had the impression of being in an airy aquarium filled with sleeping lumpfish.

I was very tired. I drifted with my blanket, my towel and cleanser down to the far end, my head as though navigating through a school of stars. An older woman with pleated eyes was sitting on the floor, resting her shoulder against a fire extinguisher, holding a bottle of beer.

"Sit down," she said, and so I did.

"Do you know," I said, "how much it costs to keep an archer in arrows?"

She snorted.

And that was all. She leaned against her fire extinguisher, and I leaned against her, and we drank and drank her smuggled beer. Eventually, she blew out so hard her lips vibrated, and then she got to her feet, pulling me up with her. We shuffled together into the john, settled into adjacent stalls, and crack! the sound of our micturitions rang out into the night like gunfire. On and on I peed. I was dreaming, this couldn't be me, this equine jet, my kidneys would surely fail, they would turn into dry knots, my skin into paper. I was terrified, I was laughing and laughing, we were both laughing and we could not stop.

When suddenly the stall door banged open, an enraged, shadowy she-walrus stood in the doorway, a thick, fingered flipper made for me, burst open my cheek. Small mercies, I thought, for my astonished bladder choked shut its flow at last.

There were other walruses outside arguing with my older woman in a gurgly english language unknown to me.

And then they had slid off back to their broken sleep, my older woman was helping me off the toilet, coocoorooing sharply, because clots of laughter continued still to heave drily in my throat, we paddled, lamely, me, my older woman, my strange face, and I, together into bed, at last, my cheek, she said, would be every, come and get me, Nick, I thought, come and get me, just look at me, Nick, I'm every, your cheek, she said, will be every, every colour, of the rainbow.

I might have been ten or eleven when my father took me to see the doctor.

"I would tend to suspect a physiological cause for her behaviour, allergies perhaps, or asthma. It might be dietary. I'd like to have her tested for lactose intolerance. It's a shame you didn't have her see someone before this."

"We should have, I know. Certainly, we should have," said my father. "So you don't think she's just plain cracked?"

"Children are never just plain cracked," said the doctor. "Adults maybe. Not children."

Do you know how much it costs to keep an archer in arrows?

The year Nick finished first in the province and second in Canada, he went through $3,432 worth of arrows.

I know because the C.W.A.A. made me keep track that year. The year before I had applied for two $6,000 grants. One in the name of Nichol P. Henry. The other in the name of Henry P. Nichol. Simple.

I got them both.

The C.W.A.A. discovered my little piece of deception, not without embarassment. They agreed that I would only have to pay back ten per cent of the grant acquired fraudulently provided I kept a documented accounting the following year to demonstrate why I needed so much money. Sweet of them. The resulting expense account for Nick's archery –

equipment, travel, range time, club dues, tournament fees, chocolate bars – came to well over $17,000. Even so, I was never granted more than $8,000 by the C.W.A.A. in that or subsequent seasons. And of course, once Nick achieved senior status, I was no longer eligible for C.W.A.A. funding at all.

This is a young man who had – who had – definite Olympic potential.

The things I've sold to keep him shooting. Fruit trees, Chelsea flatware, drafting tables, bath poufs, leaves of cheese, glow-in-the-dark jig-saw puzzles – I'm serious, depicting the night sky and constellations, very attractive really, and highly educational. I still have some if you're interested.

No house, no savings, no RRSP's.

Of course there's the darling little dye-guns. Remind me to tell you about the dye-guns.

Nick and Tibor Farkas were brothers-in-arms. Tibor had biblical cheeks, and a molded lip over which sprouted, already at fourteen, a dry, palestinian-blue moustache. His leaky eyes gave the impression of being well-adapted to reading by moonlight. He was terrified of me.

Nick announced one day that he and Tibor were going to shoot in the Provincials. They started practising together like mad. And then, one day, Nick was sitting in the kitchen as sad as nails saying how the draw had been made up and how he and Tibor would have to shoot against each other in the second round and wouldn't both be able to qualify for the Provincials after all, and how they'd gone to see Mr. Jakanax but he said he couldn't change the draw. And so on.

They went on practising like mad together, but now it

was to expiate their grief. I observed Nick closely. I knew perfectly well he was capable of letting Tibor beat him, out of friendship.

So on the day before their match, I said I'd take the two of them out for barbecued chicken, and then I had my hair straightened. I decided I looked too much like a Peruvian Indian who ate black potatoes, so I went back and had it cut short. This was much better. In my charcoal jumpsuit and red pelerine cape, and with a little predacious eyework, I looked the perfect hooded, blood-stained, crow.

This left me, however, with barely enough time to crush all the aspirins, stir in the sugar, and slide the mixture into the little yellow drawstring sack that I had acquired with my Nina Ricci body powder, before the boys arrived and we set off together.

They were as morose and silent during the meal as the barbecued chicken they were eating. I sat, as I had intended, very close to Tibor, not, as I had intended, to intimidate him with my corvine sheen, but, in fact, because I badly needed the strength of his presence to carry it off. I was trembling so rapidly, I was dizzy with nervousness, and his bare arm beside me was so still, his abstracted manner of eating so reassuring, and his dreamy affection for Nick so solid. I ordered him coffee after the meal without asking if he wanted it, and, for Nick, yet another giant Pepsi.

"I can't for the life of me," I said, "remember what the capital of Nebraska is. Go get the map book in the car, why don't you, Nick."

"Tibor'll go," said Nick.

"Nick . . .," I said.

"I'll go," said Tibor.

"Nick'll go," I said. And off Nick went, frowning, balancing a spoon on the tip of his index finger.

I took out my little yellow sack then.

"Artificial sweetener," I said. "Would you like some, Tibor?"

I poured the contents of the sack into his cup, all but a half teaspoonful or so which I poured into my own. My pulse fluttered in my lip as I stirred his coffee for him. I felt like one of those violent flowers which bursts open instantly in nature films, I was struck, suddenly, by the fetid swampland air, I heard the whish of red insects with complex wings investigating me.

Aspirin is what? $2.59 a bottle? I was just playing, wasn't I.

At any rate, Tibor was in the hospital by 4 AM. The early hour might be thought of as indicating a somewhat excitable reaction on the part of his parents. There was, apparently, a little blood in his vomit.

And Nick qualified for the Provincials. He didn't win that year, although he did win, if I'm not mistaken, the next six years in a row.

I watched him as he stood aiming, so still, so solid on the legs he was forever strengthening. I slid into the arrow's cockpit, belted myself in, strained at the controls to keep the arrow on course during the fraction of a second of flight time as the target hurtled toward me. The jolt of impact made my throat bang against the back of my neck.

I have never been sick, with a disease. I have never suffered any real pain. I have no doubt that I will live till I'm ancient and die in a brief burst of energy, like a cheap lightbulb. I have no doubt. I love to lie in the dark, in my ten-pound pyjamas, to feel and to listen as my gleaming intestines hum and mill, to uncover my pulse beating raptly just inside my Achilles tendon, in the root of my nose, under my coccyx, or to glide through the eddies of sensation, oh, well beneath my little blind nipples, deeper even than the end of my uterus. I imagine my own creamy kidneys, my succulent liver. I love my insides. I am chic, an elegant machine. Stunning.

Narcissus, flimsy soul that he was, should not have been either young, or gorgeous, or a man. He should have been chewy, middlingly agèd, and a woman. Secure in the knowledge that no outsider would love her, ever.

But back to Tibor.

I visited him the following day in the hospital. The corridors were stifling. I found him sitting on the edge of his frame bed, dressed and with his boots on, waiting to leave, his lips plump and chapped from the dry hospital air.

"How are you feeling?"

He shrugged.

"Too bad you couldn't shoot."

He shrugged again. "Nick would have beat me."

"Not necessarily."

"Yes necessarily. I was going to let him if I had to. But I wouldn't have had to."

It was barely 5:30, already pitch dark outside, and cold.

The street cats would be waking, stretching their arthritic limbs, licking the sand out of their oily paws, the black city fumes curdling their empty stomachs.

"I ralphed too, you know. Not as much as you."

All part of the plan.

"Nick told me," said Tibor. "He phoned me to say he won."

I know, I thought. I dialled.

I was so hot in my coat. I could feel the perspiration running out of my new short hair, and down my neck.

"No more barbecued chicken for us for a while, I guess."

"They don't cook it enough," said Tibor. "You can get salmonella from chicken. Not just pork."

"Can you."

Well, Tibor, I thought, we all have to make sacrifices for Nichol P., I'm afraid. I am afraid.

"Listen, Tibor," I said, "I'm sweating like a salmon in here, and I guess you're all set to go – your mother's coming is she? – so I'm going to head out."

I had to keep telling myself as I hurried away that no one would suspect anything. It was common enough for people to be seen rushing through hospitals, crying. There was no need for alarm.

So the tests were done and, as it turned out, I was not able to properly metabolize the sugar constituent in milk. Lactose.

On the whole, though, I think my father would have preferred me to be just plain cracked. He could not accept that milk, the very first white-toothed food, was in any way responsible for my, as he put it, indulgent temper. He wanted me to be guilty. Still more, he wanted to be guilty himself.

My mother, though, latched on to lactose intolerance like a baby to a pacifier. She could suck on it for hours, never tiring of telling her friends how difficult it was to keep milk out of my diet, especially with the other children being normal.

In fact, there always was, or almost always, "just a drop of" milk in the mashed potatoes, or cheese sauce half-heartedly scraped off the cauliflower. My mother was forever forgetting to order the lactose-free milk which her grocery store did not stock regularly but was able to get for her. And inevitably, inevitably, if we did have lactose-free milk in the house, we ran out of regular milk, and I would have to watch as the special, dark brown carton poured its contents out over heaping bowls of breakfast cereal.

After which I would have to listen as my father made everybody thank me for letting them use my milk.

And Death too. Death isn't some scrawny, lurking spy just waiting to slash away with his chipped scythe. I've seen Death. Death is a woman, too. A young woman.

"Hello, Mrs. Henry," she said.

All the time Nick was going to high school, *quite* a number of years in other words, I was terrified of two things: drugs, and bimbos dreaming of skiwear and white oak cupboards. I needn't have bothered. His lack of interest in drugs resulted in Nick's never touching them. His lack of interest in girls resulted in his touching hundreds. If I met Nick after school for a hamburger, he might have a bimbo with him, or he might have two. He didn't introduce them, didn't even talk to them.

He talked to me.

I asked him once what he did talk about when he talked to girls.

"Oh," he said, pausing, pouting, "life."

"Hello, Mrs. Henry," she said. "My name is Joanna. I think it's wonderful, all you've done for Nick. I admire you."

I was eating barbecue chips and she, she was standing in the kitchen doorway, her arms wrapped around a white leather sports bag, very tall and plain-eyed, with a flat face, and a smile like a mosquito. She looked directly at me for several seconds, and then she was gone. I heard her talking with Nick, heard the front door close.

I think it's wonderful. Nobody had ever told me that.

I hated her. How could she know what I had done, what I was still doing, for Nick. She who was bright and appealing and young. I hated her. It was humiliating to be put in a position where I could not help but feel gratitude.

Because I did feel gratitude. Nobody had ever told me that. And she was so bright and young, her forehead so full of projects. As young and appealing as a peeling birch, I thought, and the words rolled stupidly around in my head for hour upon hour.

I was going to tell you about the dye-guns.

Derek Thibodeau put me on to them. We went for ice-cream together during a *Lotus 1-2-3* course. I licked my Apple-achian Mountain (mounds of maple ice-cream topped with chunky applesauce), and he, in his shimmering grey suit and dark V-neck sweater, told me about how much difficulty he was having telemarketing his dye-guns. He obviously believed in the product, which shot an indelible but harmless green dye. The idea was to stain the clothing of thieves, rapists and other assailants in order to be able subsequently to identify them. It was intended, of course, for women.

Now I will sell anything. Derek gave me 52 contact names and addresses established from his telequestionnaire. I sold 37 guns.

"It can't be!" he said. "How . . . did you sell . . . thirty-seven?"

But I wouldn't tell him.

Derek's long gone now, and there's zillions of dye-guns in purses everywhere. I don't know if any have ever gone off. A fad. I expect the bottom to fall out any time now.

Aim for the eyes, I tell them. Forget the dib-dab on the shirt cuff or the seat of the pants. Imagine your aggressor trying to hide with his face covered with green slime. It won't harm him, it won't even hurt him, but it won't come off either. Aim for the eyes.

Money. *Yes*.

Although every time I hand over my credit card, which I do now with considerable frequency, a few small bubbles of mockery, of disgust, pop in my heart.

Joanna. She was pretty much constantly underfoot. She cooked for us, did dishes, laundry. You don't have time, Mrs. Henry. No, but I didn't like her saying so. She was older than Nick, studying physical education at university. And she wanted Nick to go to university after the Commonwealth

Games. Nick, who was shaving by the time he got out of grade school.

She would say: Many students who do poorly in high school do well in university. Yes, I would say, but Nick wasn't a poor student, he was a terrible one. He has a learning disability. He's a dummy. If Nick's a dummy, there's lots of dummies in university. He just needs to learn to work. He needs encouragement. Work! All he thinks about is nocking another $25 carbon arrow into his $1,500 bow. You're right, you know. He loves archery.

And he's good at it.

I could not get her to stop admiring me. I dug up all the dirt I could about myself. I told her I was cheap and ill-tempered, that I was banned from half the grocery stores in town, that I had been to jail. She admired me all the more. And I, for my trouble, simply fell into the habit of talking to her, of looking forward to talking to her.

We were staying in a hotel during one of Nick's tournaments. We had crossed several time zones, we were too tired and disoriented to eat, but we had to go down anyway and meet him at the banquet. We bumped each other in the narrow bathroom, sucked in our stomachs, held in our behinds in order to move about between the sink and the shower. Joanna had forgotten her eye make-up so she borrowed mine, asked me what shade would suit her and proceeded to use the same shade as I had. The result was so hideous that she thought the only remedy would be to put on the same orange cheek blush, and then the same heavy lipstick, so that we ended up looking surprisingly like each other, like two common clowns. We were a little giddy, we made faces together in the mirror to check the brightness of our teeth, and Joanna said: "Some girls are A-cups, some girls are B-cups. Us . . . we're eggcups."

It seemed very funny that evening. We hardly dared to look at each other during dinner. It didn't help that there were deviled eggs in the salad. And afterwards, when Nick had gone up to bed, we sat behind a spiky plant in the lobby, and watched bustlines go by.

I remember it was very windy. I was to show a house in the afternoon. Joanna had promised she would be back in time to go with me. She and Nick were out looking for furniture. They were moving into an apartment together.

I went into Nick's room. There was the poster of a hockey player named Williams which must have been fifteen years old and which I had acquired for him because I thought every boy wanted a poster of a hockey player. Every time we moved I put it up in his new bedroom. I guess he liked it. He never took it down.

The ribbons and trophies were in boxes in his closet.

There was a folding cot for Joanna.

There was a book holding the window open. Nick could not sleep unless the door was closed and the window was open. I closed the window. There was a telephone number written on the cover of the book. A phone number, a date, and the initials, "C. L."

Now this intrigued me, because the rendez-vous in question had taken place since the time when Nick's every move had to meet with Joanna's approval. He couldn't have been touching bimbos behind her back, could he? I dug out his archery log and learned that on that particular day, he had run three miles, done 130 sit-ups, and shot 250 rounds. But he had not seen anyone with the initials "C. L." Not in connection with archery.

So I spent a very long half an hour going through all the Ls in the phone book, found nothing, and ate a box of eggrolls.

And then I had the bright idea of looking through the bills that Joanna made me put into big brown envelopes now that she was keeping my books for the accountant. And there it was, the phone number, the very one, on the optometrist's bill. The bill, that is, for contact lenses.

I should have remembered. I gave them to him after I sold my three-thousandth dye-gun or something. Joanna told me he wanted them. I guess he liked them. He wore them.

I had two hours to wait until Joanna got back. It was so hot and stuffy, and I was starting to perspire.

As it turned out though, I only had one hour to wait. They arrived together. Windy with happiness.

"You won't be*lieve*," squealed Joanna, "all the stuff. Listen listen listen listen listen!"

They had gone to a used furniture store. A junk store. The owner was dressed in a crumpled black suit, a fur hat, and twenty at least years of beard. They had looked around nervously, found a sofa. Two hundred dollars, said the beard. They could get a new sofa, thought Joanna, at a discount store for not much more than that. Two hundred dollars, said the beard. They were just pushing the door open to leave, when the voice, barely heavier than a shadow, said, Wait. I have lamps. He had two carved wooden lamps, one a moose, the other a boy leaning against a lamppost. Nick loved them. Sofa and lamps, two hundred dollars. Well, no thanks all the same. Wait. I have chairs. He came back with four bundles of sticks wrapped in string. You glue, you clamp, he said. You varnish. Brand new chairs, made to look old. Like . . . like this one there. Brand new. Two hundred dollars. Sofa, lamps, chairs. Well . . . okay, we'll take them. Wait, said the voice, I have mix-masters.

They were brimming over with happiness. Their two hundred dollars had bought them enough junk to start their own store. And I was so glad they were there that I wished Joanna would forget about the house we were supposed to show. So glad I could have screamed at them. So glad I wished they would abandon me right then and there.

We left Nick phoning to rent a truck, I remember that, and I remember stopping as we always did at the bakery to buy some hot rolls to put in our purses so the house we were trying to sell would smell enticingly of fresh bread, but I do not, I do not remember getting back in. I do not remember the expressway. I remember I was in an arrow hurtling towards the target, I remember a roaring in my ears which might well have been the people in the stands standing, I remember the jolt of impact which made my voice bang against the back of my neck.

But I do not remember . . . anything . . . real.

I remember it was very windy.

And I remember death. I've seen death. Death, you see, is a woman, a young woman, she has a long body, angular and taut, harmonious. She flows among us, energetic, although not hasty. She admires us.

She wants us so much to like her.

My mother fed on my temper, didn't she. I needed her. Obviously. How could anyone flailing away on the floor like a pinched beetle and shrieking loud enough to melt a stone not need help. A tapeworm, though, does not nibble out so much of the insides of its host that the host out-and-out dies. No, no. Parasites must be subtle, self-disciplined. My mother was my parasite. She needed to help me; therefore, she did not want to cure me.

My father was my meek predator, my oilbird, my goat-sucker. He flapped around in my temper, getting redder and redder, holding me down as I squealed and spat, trying to outsquawk me, until, with my gooey rage still clinging to his bill and his bent feathers, he plumped off awkwardly, miserable, looking for some dark corner to lick his wings, alone.

Between the two of them, they ate me up.

Nick's gone. He does not believe I cannot remember if I was driving. He says if I can't remember it means I was. He told me so. That and some other things that he shouldn't have said to his mother. His soul is broken.

He thinks I hated Joanna. He said so. I can't remember. The first person who got to me found me walking in a daze down the expressway. I had lost my voice. I don't remember.

All I remember is seeing Joanna's long body. They had pulled her out of the back seat. She couldn't have been sitting in the back.

I couldn't have.

I just couldn't.

Nick's gone. I can't stay here.

I'm going home. My father has glaucoma. My mother's immense.

Won't they have fun digesting their lactose-intolerant daughter.

YOU, JUDITH KAMADA

I was, you see, a larcenist. I did not belong in university. I didn't go. I stayed in my apartment.

My father had paid my fees. I could hear him calling me. Calling me with my own voice. Judy! *Judy!* Calling me a thief.

But I could not match the nervous palaver of the hippiettes with their hair like strands of tinted glass, thick and sweet with pot smoke. They did not go to their classes either, but they belonged.

The cream-coloured walls of my apartment were stained with the voices of previous occupants, their pleas, their pleasures. The hide-a-bed mattress was crusty with their mucosal secretions, the bathroom smelled of their humid hair. They were my antecedents, if not my ancestors. Their presence was welcome.

A Nigerian giantess from down the hall asked me to tutor her daughter whose skin was so dark I felt sure it would leave a mark when she touched me. To my disappointment, it did not. This job led to others. I was, as a university student, assumed to know everything and I always said yes. So that I was soon spending my mornings learning what I was supposed to teach in the afternoon.

There was a bookseller where I bought or traded piles of books. The owner took back my texts at almost full price. He was my reserve. He could always negotiate a transaction that resulted in his giving me money.

And then.

And then winter came, I suppose. The heat had to be paid before the tutor. Only the Nigerian girl kept coming, with her skin like potting soil mixed with butter, and she was far cleverer than I was or ever had been. My bookseller bought back all the books that his inverted sense of business permitted. The rest he took on consignment. That is, he put them in a box on a table staggering already under its load of such boxes.

I left a letter at the registrar's office by which I withdrew from the university, and after that, I rattled through the city streets, the sun a slice of raw potato floating in the steaming sky. I walked for days, my stomach churned with hunger, my sides split with cold, but my vital organs were insulated well enough by the brittle foam of my anonymity.

One morning the phone rang. It was my bookseller. He had a customer with him who was interested in one of my books, *The Poetics of Vehement Disorder*, an obscure piece of unreadability about which I remember only that the author was a Russian anarchist, Usakanov his name was, Alexei, and that the introduction contained an exhortation to all comrades of conscience to throw the book away after reading it, and to all comrades of courage to simply throw it away. The bookseller asked me how much I thought I wanted, seeing as it was a difficult book to obtain.

"I don't know," I said into the phone. "$3.49."

"Seventeen dollars?" he answered. I heard him repeat this figure to the customer.

"The gentleman is agreeable," said the bookseller. "He is going to wait for you here at the store."

The gentleman's name was Michael Leicester. He was talking to the bookseller when I arrived, and without interrupting his conversation or even paying much attention to me, he managed to give me the seventeen dollars and the impression that I was to wait for him.

"I own a small grocery store," he said when we were outside, "on Fairmont Street. If you need a job, you can work there. I can only pay you minimum wage. A little more maybe."

I attempted unsuccessfully to speak.

"Oh," he said quickly, "you don't have to say yes right now. Or no. Just show up when and if you want to."

And so I began to work at the grocery store, making pyramids of oranges, mopping the floor, doing the cash. Every evening at six I locked the door and began to walk. There was nothing inventive or exploratory about my walking. I was like a clown walking in front of a screen onto which are projected drawings of crooked buildings, with the difference that the clown casts a shadow onto the screen. I walked until I was too tired to walk any more, climbed up to my apartment, ate some toast that I made on the stove with a bent hanger, and fell asleep.

Michael Leicester was never at the grocery store. I had

not even seen him since the bookseller's, a fact which did not prevent, which no doubt encouraged, his constant presence beside me, suggesting I turn the tomato cans to all face the same way, sighing at the flat-faced mothers palpating every lettuce, observing sideways the light-eyed, dark-fingered children.

Counterfeiter, said I to myself. Bald-faced forger. To print his face on your play money, simply because he showed two bit's worth of interest in you, a mere modicum.

Still, the grocery store was the pin of my existence. I arrived earlier and earlier. The diameter of my trudgings shrank until I was rarely out of eyeshot of its baying, moon-black windows.

There was a storeroom behind the grocery. One night, quite late, as I leaned against the wall under the storeroom window, too tired to keep walking but not yet cold enough to go home, I heard voices talking with animation. And although I could not make out what the voices were saying, I knew that one of them was Michael Leicester's.

I listened for a long time, as I might have listened to a recording of a grass fire. I returned every night, and every night, or almost, the storeroom discussions crackled distantly under the window.

And then it was Michael himself bursting into the grocery one evening at six.

"Closing time," he said, all vinegar and vim. "Where would you like to go for dinner?"

He decided I would like to go somewhere where they served smoked meat. After the quarried beef had been brought, he asked me, amid much oversized chewing, a number of anodine questions about myself. And then: "So what have you found out so far?"

The pointed impetus of his tone brought the belligerance to my cheeks. "What do you mean what have I found out?"

"I know you've been observing us. I would just like to know why."

"I have not been observing anybody."

"I am to suppose then that you stand in the cold and eavesdrop for fun."

"I don't. . . ." My combativeness melted, realizing instantly as I did that Michael was a man who could never really know me, who could never wear the colour-scheme of my nature.

"I wasn't eavesdropping," I said.

"You were just curious then."

"No, I was not just-curious-then." And after a time, "I'll find another job."

"Do so."

And you, said I, and you, when you grope in the dark, is it for something other than the light switch? For something other than something to make the dark go away? We are all moths, we all spend our lives banging stupidly into street lamps while the whole, gentle, welcoming darkness waits. And if the storeroom discussions are my glim, what of it? And even if I say storeroom discussions when what I mean is your voice, and even if I say glim when what I mean is. . . . It reassures me, there I've said it, plain and simple. Your voice reassures me, what of that? What is there in that that gives you the right to observe me?

"Unless," he said into my fulminating silence, "you would like to join us."

He pulled out his, formerly my, copy of *The Poetics*, opened it, read selected excerpts of the type: "The temptations of God have always done more to undermine man's moral nature than the temptations of Satan." And: "The greatest danger for the revolutionary is to seek peace, not with his assailants, but with himself." And so on.

"Those are all passages you underlined," he said. "Why?"

Satan, thought I, Old Gooseberry. And did well to do so, seeing as you are now reading them to me.

"I was researching a paper," I said, "on grandiloquent Russian sophistry."

He looked at me hard for a moment through the plexiglass panel that shot up between us, and then gathered his coat to leave.

"I could . . . ," I said, observing the salty French fry bits left on his plate, "I would like to join you."

And so began my brief time if not on the outskirts, certainly not among the inner crinolines either, of Marxism-Leninism as a revolutionary's apprentice. There were two others with Michael, one named Dan, I forget the other one's name. Dan I remember because of his half-finger gloves and choker scarves. And because, so he said, he had sat at Marx's desk in the British Museum.

I continued in the grocery store during the day, and after hours I did whatever I could to be useful. There being no shortage of things to do.

Pamphlets. I mimeographed them endlessly and passed them out at subway entrances, feeling each one slip from my hand as today earth slips from my hand to cover a tulip bulb. And when the police told me to move along, I astonished myself by berating them with all the brassy recalcitrance of the unconvinced. Which did not please Michael. "Just disappear," he would say. "Did they follow you?"

Follow me. Me. For whom what was behind was a void. Something I never considered, that slipped around in back of me whenever I myself turned around. To think of this void as peopled with following eyes offended me, thrilled me.

There was always a picket line or a student demonstration somewhere to be driven to in Michael's Volvo station wagon. I was often not sure who to root for at these events, student activists being usually, though not always, more despised even than capitalists. In any case, my principal function was that of deposit box for all the bits of paper with names and addresses that Michael gathered.

Above all, I organized courses, two at least every week, that took place in elementary school rooms with poster paintings and miniature desks, the school authorities, thanks to me, under the impression the course was about life insurance, the lecturer one of Michael's innumerable American friends flown up from New York or Detroit to expound historical materialism, say, or dialectics and the arts to the five sullen drill press operators with doughnut sugar on their lips that I had managed to talk into showing up during interminable phone conversations.

Much of all this was done in the storeroom, at my vegetable-crate desk. Too often against the background of the grass fire discussions, which were not as soothing listened to from close range. Intense, argumentative and mirthless, they revolved around the wording of a long document Michael was preparing, an ambitious plan for the progressive infiltration of the party. I did not have the theoretic equipment to follow all that was said, or shouted, but I understood well enough that the plan called for highly disruptive social action, too much so for Dan and the other.

As the weeks went by, Michael became more and more agitated, while Dan and the other were less and less often to be seen.

One night, very late, I was typing the manuscript which Michael desperately wanted to finish, and which he was afraid, desperately, to finish. He was very tired, although I was not. I never was, in his company. I extorted his energy, no doubt, and burned it up myself.

"You should get to bed," he said. "You're tired."

He set up a folding cot on which I lay down as instructed, and then he turned out all the lights except for the one at his desk and resumed working.

After a time he said, "I don't know if we're going to make it."

"Mmn?" said I.

"The word is the RCMP is out to nail us."

"Buy them," I said, like a pro, having seen Michael on more than one occasion give money to policemen. He laughed a noisy, humourless laugh.

"You can get out while the getting's good if you like," he said.

"I don't like."

"Well watch yourself then, Judith."

This comment, which contained his one and only ever nominal reference to me, and which today tightens my throat with a nostalgia that is surely a form of grief, did not, at the time, please me.

"Just get your paper written," I said. "I'll look after myself."

Again he laughed. Silently this time, but with humour.

Until the morning when I arrived to find the grocery store crouching under a fringe of giant icicles like meaty, glass parsnips, the windows covered with plywood sheets, the green paint peeling and black. I did not stop. The air had been sucked from my lungs through a hard tube in my throat, I expected every instant some plainclothes behemoose to block my way, to say my name from behind, "You, Judith Kamada!" I rode on buses for hours, terrified the police would be waiting for me at my apartment, my legs mewling as I crept up the stairs at last, craning my neck to catch sight of them before they me.

But they were not there.

No, I whimpered, childish in my bed, the grocery store matters enough to be burnt to a crisp, but I do not matter enough even to be questioned.

After that I stayed in my room, so saturated with loneliness I could not move. It stiffened all my joints, its narcotic fumes were in my nose and mouth, putting me to sleep for days on end.

It is when I am most separated from my life that I feel most alive. When my life is most like me, like a lifeless sweater I have been wearing for years, and hating, I have no desire to act or be acted on. And here I was wearing, hating, the absurd hope (me all over!) that I would hear footsteps in the corridor, that Michael Leicester would stop in front of my door, while my smug skin was cold all over with the opinion that I would never hear from him again.

Do not believe those who think they know what is happening to you. I and my skin were both wrong.

The footsteps came, the knock. My pulse soared, I could feel it in my palm as I opened the door.

"Judith Kamada?" she said.

Oh, I thought, a shiver passing through me, who *are* you? Her forehead was shiny with fever, her eyes were glazed. You are my twin. Not of who I am, but of who I would have liked to have been. You have stolen my one chance at being beautiful. She sat on my sofa, very self-contained, mute, almost prim.

"I'm not feeling very well," she said to explain her silence. And then, "I have a letter for you from Michael."

She handed me the letter. I stuffed it into my pocket where it squirmed and nipped like a trapped crayfish.

"Would you like some macaroni dinner?" I said.

She ate slowly, talking to me confidingly, restlessly, assuming I was a longtime communist, an error I did nothing to correct, mentioning many names I had never heard while I scrunched my forehead to appear concerned. Although I was concerned. So many people lying low, moving away.

I was seized, offended, by her viperine contempt for those die-easy party members who had scurried for shelter at some suburban cousin's.

"It is not possible to make revolution," she said, her ill eyes sparkling with disdain, "not here, not in this wingless country."

She curled up on the sofa, her back to me, and went to sleep.

The letter was addressed to "J. Kamada." In it Michael said that the person bearing the letter was quote an important human being unquote, and that, although I was under no obligation to do so and he would perfectly understand if I refused, he would consider it a personal service if I quote lent unquote her my passport. He looked forward to seeing me again once things quieted down.

I am still looking forward to seeing him again. I say that without sarcasm.

I always will.

She woke some time later, a gust of panic blowing over her face until she rememebered where she was.

"Why are you looking at me?" she said.

Because you have stolen my one chance.

"Oh," I said, "I was picturing you in . . . in foreign capitals, Rangoon, Buenos Aires, Budapest, Paree. I think you should go to all of them at least once."

She took my hands then in hers which were burning and limp. I drew my hands away, and took hers in mine.

And we never mentioned Michael Leicester again.

Oh she was weepy and exhausted and got substantially crankier before she got better, but she put the hep back into my step, the glide back into my stride. I had never had anyone to look after, I went out and bought real food, pored over chickens, palpated every lettuce, returned to find my apartment bulging with her bed-ridden odour, as though a kilo of frozen lichen had been put in the oven at 425° for seven or eight minutes. Is it possible, thought I, that I too smell so pungent in another's nose.

One day she got up and made some tea, drank half, hurled the cup across the room, threw open the fire escape door and stepped out into the persistent rain that was shriveling the snow and eating into the sidewalks. She stayed out long enough to become thoroughly wet, re-entered and said: "You're going to do something for me."

She opened an exercise book full of names and addresses, and soon she had me running all over town, trick-or-treating, knocking on doors, meeting men in bars and beside shopping mall fountains, canvassing for money. There were those who claimed to have never heard of her, those who gave a few, and more than a few dollars, hoping no doubt it would buy their release from all further soliciting, and those who handed me thick, sealed envelopes.

She told me to take my passport to the offices of a certain small-town newspaper. I got on a new bus that aspirated its way into the country where the fields were drying out in the crisscross spring winds. It dropped me off in a town made of bricks. I soon found the local paper.

"What are *you* doing here?" said an irritated voice the instant I entered. "As if I didn't know."

It was Dan, wearing shirt-sleeve garters and a visor. He took the passport and told me to come back in two days.

Which I did. He was quite drunk this time. He fanned himself with the passport that now contained her picture instead of mine, saying that Michael owned several other small grocery stores, that it was easy to be a communist when you were floating in equity, that maybe the RCMP arranged to have the Fairmont Street store incinerated and maybe Michael arranged it himself, that, in any case, the only reason he had taken an interest in *me* was because I resembled *her* and seemed pliable enough to get a passport out of. And so on.

"Yes," I said, "but you're not telling me anything I don't already know. Michael asked me about the passport long before I worked at the store."

I plucked the black booklet out of his hand and left, invigorated by the joy of lying.

A few days later, we bought her an airline ticket together.

And then she was standing in my doorway, shouting, "I'm leaving now!" at me, who was out on the sunny fire escape, unable to answer, unable to move. She walked back through the apartment, said, sharply, "Everything will go fine," and left. I waited and waited, but nothing happened. No sirens, no commotion, no crack snipers surrounding my building. No, no. Everything went fine.

Fine. Everything did go fine. I waited and waited. But she did not change her mind. She did not come back. I received a postcard of O'Hare airport. Unsigned. On the back she had written, "Thanks."

But I, had I made any attempt to convince her to stay? No. She was, what was she? She was inaccessible, superb, she knew how to move, to manoeuvre, she knew what to do with names and addresses, she could get people to get her money and passports.

She set me up. She stole my one chance. And I was glad she did. Having no more chances, I could just do the life gig, get married, work, miscarry, work, learn Windows, convince my husband to buy a Volvo station wagon.

I walked around and around for years with a picture of her buried among the crumbs and grains of dirt in the bottom of my purse. For years.

While each day deposited its layer of forgetful sediment. I even managed to forget her name. Ca . . .? Carol? No. Karen? Perhaps. I don't remember.

Layer upon languid layer, with just a thin little green crust, where I plant my crocuses.

Ah, but the earth has more faults than a human heart even. It shudders and cracks its toes while our wee overpasses buckle and we scream. Real beanstalks burst through back yards overnight and bring down giants that can breathe in blood.

Messages from Dayton appear on my screen :

judy, i post you verbatim this small terrifying piece from today's paper – police found the body of a woman yesterday in a cambridge park apartment. the landlord who was owed several months rent had requested police assistance after the woman failed repeatedly to answer her door. the cause of death is unclear although the woman was apparently suffering from severe malnutrition. found on the premises was a long-expired canadian passport in the name of judith kamada. thought it was you kid for half a half a second. any other j k's living up there? the piss right out of scared me it did nearly.

Look at me. Do you see me shake?

What has become of me? The life gig. The unhurried pursuit of a not-too-distant happiness. Is that not enough?

I cannot imagine what events could have led to such misery. I have not the intensity, the breadth of experience. She never got in touch with me. Never. I could not have known. I am not guilty of manslaughter. I am not. I am not. I am not.

THE HOUSEHOLD CUP

He stood on the platform, looking steadily at a series of numbers painted down the side of the train coach.

He did not look up at the windows. In part because he had said, "Goodbye then, good life," and she had said, "Goodbye, good . . . bye," so that he did not now want to catch sight of her by chance. But also because it did not seem appropriate, in view of the joyless circumstances, to appear interested in the expectant commotion of passengers settling into train seats. Or, certainly, to leave the platform before the train had pulled out. So he stood and stared at the numbers, familiar, clear, meaningless.

He was aware of a voice calling, aware that it had been calling for some time. He could hear its insistance, its exasperation. Who is it, he thought, who is not answering?

"Hatchman! John Hatchman!"

John Hatchman, he thought, must be deaf.

"Haatchmaaaan!"

He glanced up. A woman was hanging dangerously far out of the next coach. She was wearing a green hat with a feather, and she was looking at him.

"*Fin*ally!" she said.

Her mouth was as wide-brimmed as her hat. She appeared convivial, corn-fed.

"I was beginning to think it wasn't youuuuu!"

Her enthusiasm overreached her equilibrium, and down she swung, her forehead banging against the side of the coach, her hair dangling, the green hat dropping to the ground. Hands shot out of the window and hauled her back in. The window was banged shut, sealing him again in silence.

The train grunted then, shuddered through its entire length, and undertook its lugubrious advance.

And he returned to the apartment where he had been living for some time, although not, until this day, alone. The air was so thick there, so gelatinous, that he could feel it sliding into his throat. He could feel the mirrors about to burst, the standing lamps about to buckle and crash. He could hear the floor straining to contain the condensed weight of the furniture.

He could not stay there. He rode on buses, wandered through stores. He went into the mens' room at the Y to weep, but his tears were cowed by the blatant sounds in the neighbouring stalls. He visited a museum that was being renovated, saw, against the white walls, the still whiter shadows of paintings that had been taken down, and he knew he was looking at himself.

He entered a restaurant and walked down the aisles, stooping to look through the windows as if the restaurant were a passenger jet cruising through the summer streets. He found himself in front of the pay phone, leafing through the directory, looking up, "Hatchman." His eye was caught by "Hatchman's Barber Shop" printed in heavy letters. But there were no other entries. None. So instead of simply closing the phone book as he would surely have done had there been fifty or even five Hatchmans, he dialled the one number which seemed to have been expressly intended for his discovery.

"Hello," said a voice.

"Hello," he said, pausing. "This is John."

"John? Not John Hatchman!"

"Yes."

"Oh, but that's great! It'll make Harold happy to see you, John. You haven't met me. My name's Peter."

"How do you do."

"So, when are you going to drop by the shop and see us? Harold's sleeping right now. Later on, say."

"Sure."

So that that evening he was standing behind a streetlamp and telephone pole erected side by side, observing Hatchman's Barber Shop, in an old part of the city, without history or charm, simply old, the street damp and confined, the facing stone walls so permeated with shade that it oozed out of their pores and ran down in black streaks.

Tantalized though he was by the patient gloom of the shop he had been watching now for several hours, he could not summon the nerve to cross the street. He was agitated and very hungry, his scalp itched, fleeting pains squeezed his rib cage, leaving him oddly relieved. His lungs, he thought, must be moulting.

A seagull glided unsteadily through the open strip of darkening sky above him. It swerved shakily, crashed into the telephone pole and tumbled earthward. Reviving in mid-fall, it shivered its addled wings, flapped with frenetic nonchalance, and lugged itself skyward.

And he, having jumped into the street to avoid the gull, found himself face to face with Hatchman's Barber Shop. The shop was already striding jerkily across the street to meet him. The dented knob of the glass door reached out for his hand, turned it, and drew him inside.

"Well now!" cried out in chorus the several voices of a single man, barrel-bodied, good-sized, his moustache trimmed with Latinate precision, his black enamel hair made, apparently, from a plastic mold. "Well now, if that's not a Hatchman my name's not Zinc. I know Harold will be happy to see you."

The man looked Hatchman frankly up and down. "Of course Zinc's not my real name." He held out his hand. "Peter Vardemaens."

After that, he lowered the door and window shades, an action that had the contradictory effect of increasing the amount of light in the barber shop, which was filled with wainscotting, creamy porcelain, swan-necked water spouts, and two red barber chairs.

"Harold's still sleeping," he said. "He sleeps more and more. Maybe because he still dreams about the things he can't remember when he's awake. Don't expect him to recognize you."

He struck a match and lit a small burner underneath a turning, mustard-coloured candle. After a moment, he ran a knife down the sides of the candle, gathering the oozy scrapings on a square of toast. This he gave to Hatchman together with a glass of beer, bid him take his place in one of the barber chairs, and tucked a sheet under his chin like a giant bib.

"There are days when a door handle perplexes Harold. I'd give anything to see him cut hair just once more. Just once. You see the froth in your glass? That's where Harold is. He doesn't know any more that he has floated up out of his beery past. He doesn't know that he will soon be tilted out and sloshed into the fleshy throat of the future. He just lives in his layer of froth. On his good days, I have the impression he remembers that he once remembered. I say good days. When he's frightened, resentful, covered in sweat. His bad days are better. He sleeps."

Hatchman sat and listened to the scissors clicking around his ears like a stiff, paper moth, he ate the mysterious wax which was in fact warm cheese, imagined he was drinking in the brew of Harold Hatchman's past.

"Harold knows," said Vardemaens, "when it's time to eat, but he doesn't remember if he will ever have to eat again. Of course we all have things to forget. It is the things we have to forget that bully us into becoming what we are. The things we remember are just decorations along the way for the most part. To forget is the prerogative of any living memory, and a privilege which Harold does not enjoy. It's not just that he can't remember. Harold can't forget."

He could feel the barber's voice going to his head. And who, he wondered, was this Harold Hatchman anyway, from what sulky deckhand descended whose job it was to man which forward hatches, when and for what reason gone ashore to barber in the street under the pink awning of which Tunisian café, the stench of sun-infested seaweed masking the shyness of his English accent in front of which passing, buttery-eyed, Muslim women, fat with the smell of peppers?

He shuddered, straightened up in his chair.

"Hmm," he said, "I very nearly fell asleep."

"You wouldn't have been the first," said Vardemaens, handing him a large slice of spiced, jellied liver.

"Can I ask you a question?"

"Certainly."

"Why did you say your name was Zinc?"

"I said my name wasn't Zinc."

"Why didn't you say that then?"

"All right, I'll tell you. But you have to tell me first about your uncle Harold. Something you remember from when you were young. Anything. I'll go get him while you think about it. Help yourself," he said, indicating the tableclothed table covered not only with raclettes, terrines, brown bottles planted in ice-pails, white bread and black, but also with more *barquettes* and cakes than were there surely when he had entered.

It did not occur to him to help himself. But it did not occur to him either to remove the sheet from under his chin, get down out of the red chair, and leave. He was as though injected with a sweet serum made by swirling the conniving delight of playing John Hatchman into the temptation of being discovered, accused of treachery, hated, humiliated.

So that he had not so much as moved a muscle when Vardemaens returned, pushing in front of him a man wearing a glowing, white undershirt, more massive even than Vardemaens himself, whose frightened, bristly hair appeared to be growing in again after having been completely shaved, and whose muscular arms and straining belly only emphasized his ill fragility.

"There he is," said Vardemaens. "That's your nephew John sitting in your chair."

"Hello," said John the nephew, as Hatchman eyed him with an eerie steadiness, the aspect of his gaze prolonging itself over several seconds without development or nuance.

"Hungry Harold?" said Vardemaens, a question that rekindled in Hatchman's eyes a small but distinct enthusiasm. He sat down at the crowded table, straightened his knife and fork, leaned to one side so Vardemaens could set in front of him a roast chicken steaming with tarragon.

Vardemaens placed a second chicken on a tray across the arms of John the nephew's chair, whispering as he did so that the more Hatchman's memory withered, the more his appetite grew.

"So," he said out loud, digging into his own chicken, holding up a drumstick like a conductor's baton, "what do you remember about your Uncle Harold?"

"Well," said John the nephew, "I didn't see Uncle Harold often, and it's a long time ago."

"Not *that* long ago," said Vardemaens. "Way you go. You can make it up if you like. We don't care."

So he began, nervous, tentative, relating incidents involving his own uncles, gaining more confidence as he met with approval and as it became clear that Vardemaens knew little if anything of Hatchman's past, and that Hatchman himself was interested only in his chicken. He became more daring, furnished more details and, "Oh yes," he said, "*That's* a good story. When we drove to Disneyland."

"Harold's been to Disneyland!" said Vardemaens.

"Yes, he has. I don't remember what kind of car he had, it was old though, and black, my parents didn't think it was roadworthy enough to cross a continent but Harold said 'you're not going to say the kid can't come, his other cousins are coming for the luva,' and so they let me go, and they were of course right because on the third day the engine reduced itself to a sniggering tablespoon of molten metal, blew off in the process enough steam to change the weather, and Harold had to dig all the bags out of the trunk and make us walk. Harold and five kids and their suitcases trundling through the knee-deep grass along the highway. When what to our wondering eyes should appear but the clacking pennants of a Ford dealership, a rollicking outpost on the tax-cheap fringe of town. There was a two-tone Meteor station wagon with a padded dash on the lot. Harold told us to get in, he went inside and he bought it, cash. I could see him through the picture window, take out a wad of bills as thick as a dictionary, pay for the car, and put back in his pocket a wad of bills as thick as a concise dictionary."

A guffaw exploded through the twin barrels of Hatchman's nose with such force that he lurched forward in order that the two blown-glass drools of mucus not dangle onto his immaculate undershirt.

"Cash!?" he said. "I, Harold Hatchman. Cash! What kind of house did I live in?"

John the nephew, dumbfounded, looked over at

Vardemaens for assurance, who at the same time looked at John the nephew, his lower lids filled with tears.

"Go on, go on," he said. "I *knew* your coming would do him good. What kind of house *did* he live in?"

"I don't *know*," stammered John the nephew. "A house house. I was only there once or twice."

Hatchman's burst of apperception attenuated itself into a luminescent stare directed at John the nephew, a scientific stare not unlike that of a two-week-old infant observing its foot. The stare gradually diminished in intensity until it died out completely, and Hatchman resumed his meal.

"I knew it would do him good," repeated Vardemaens excitedly, pouring more yellow wine into his and John the nephew's glasses. John the nephew shifted positions noisily, placed his palms decisively on his thighs, and said:

"That *was* excellent."

"Portugese," said Vardemaens, sinking his spoon into his own bowl. "Squash flan."

"*Very* good," said John the nephew. "Well now, I think it's about time for me to be."

"I've been to Disneyland," said Hatchman.

"Yes, you have, Harold," said Vardemaens.

"Yes, I have," said Hatchman. "It was eighteen dollars regular admission, eleven dollars and fifty cents for children under fourteen, and six dollars for children under seven. The sales tax was two percent on regular admission tickets. I gave the girl a hundred dollars and she gave me back seventeen dollars and twenty-eight cents change."

"I don't remember all that," said John the nephew with taut admiration.

"You don't re*mem*ber!" bellowed Hatchman. "Of course you don't remember. *You* didn't pay. Do you remember what year it was?"

"Ooo," said John the nephew, "that's tough."

"What do you mean, tough?" said Hatchman. "You were there, weren't you? It was the same year I won the Household Cup."

"Okay," said John the nephew.

"How many days were there that year?" said Hatchman.

"Three hundred and sixty-some. Five, maybe. Maybe six. Eh, Peter?"

"I won the Household Cup on the two hundred and ninety-eighth day," said Hatchman. "I know that." He hesitated then, like an ageing bear not sure of the meaning of an unfamiliar odour. He returned reluctantly to his frothy lair.

"Everyone was there," he muttered doubtfully.

"Not everyone," said John the nephew. "The attendance was twenty-three thousand eight hundred and four."

"There were more than *that*!" said Hatchman vigourously.

"No, that was the official paid attendance. Twenty-four thousand three hundred and eight."

"But there were standees, and gate crashers, and kids who climbed over the fence at the south end."

"I don't deny that. I'm only saying that the paid attendance was . . ."

"Twenty-eight thousand four hundred and three," chimed in Vardemaens, thrilled by Hatchman's vivacity.

"There were more than that," said Hatchman. "There were people climbing up the scaffolding. There were people who tied themselves to the lights."

"There was one who fell off," said John the nephew.

"One, yes," said Hatchman, "there was."

"It was a woman," said John the nephew. "She fell out of the lights with her rope attached to her waist and watched the proceedings hanging upsidedown. I say watched. So much blood flowed into her head that her nose started bleeding. The blood ran into her eyes and hair and dripped onto the asphalt below. Harold was the first to notice. He called the firemen. They couldn't get their truck into position because of all the cars blocking the way, so that by the time they got the woman down, she had a horn of hair stiff with blood sticking straight up from her head. And she was dying."

"Dying!" said Vardemaens.

"Yes," said Hatchman, "she was."

"She was unconscious and needed blood badly. But by this time, even more cars had arrived and the firemen couldn't get out. So Harold wrapped the woman's head in bags of ice cubes, put her into his Meteor station wagon, and set out for the hospital two towns away, yelling at her, in this big, black, comic strip voice, there was no one to hear him, yelling at her, 'Hey baby, don't you bleed on my front seat, don't you even dare die.'"

"Harold talks like that!" said Vardemaens.

"When no one's listening he does. 'Don't you dare die, baby. Ten-foa?'"

"Harold talks like that!" said Vardemaens. "I'll bet he does. Do it for me, Harold. Just once."

Hatchman, who was staring at John the nephew as though he, John the nephew, were on several televisions all at once, the repeated images identical and yet not the same, said, softly:

"Ten-four. Baby."

Vardemaens swallowed a yelp, opened another bottle of the cold, yellow wine and passed out handfuls of twice-cooked almond biscuits.

"So," said John the nephew, advancing his lower jaw to keep the crumbs from falling out of his mouth, "Harold gets to the hospital. The first thing the nurse does is to cut off the horn of hair, which she gives to him. The second thing is to test the girl's blood type which is V.S.O.P. 'We don't have any V.S.O.P.,' she says. Harold's an athlete. He knows his blood type. 'I do,' he says. 'You're V.S.O.P.?' says the nurse."

"I'll bet he is," said Vardemaens.

"She downloads an armful. 'Lie there twenty minutes', she says, except that the firemen and how many hundred others have got to the hospital by now, they're chanting 'Hatchman-Hatchman-Harold-*Hatch*man' so loudly they wake the girl up.

"'Are you Harold Hatchman?' she says forlornly.

"'Yes. Who're you?'

"'Pamela Vinegar?' she says uncertainly, drunk no doubt on Harold's sobering V.S.O.P. trickling down the intravenous.

"'Oh,' says Harold, his crest falling. 'Any relation to Percy?'

"'Yes,' says Pamela.

"'Oh,' says Harold, his crest falling further.

"'Hatchman-Hatchman-Harold-*Hatch*man.'

"He grabs the horn of hair and heads out. Huge cheer.

Everybody roars off to get places in the grandstand. Harold feels like death. He slides into his blue Meteor. It is almost dark now and starting to snow. Like dying he feels. She is related to Percy Vinegar.

"He drives back to the canal where the grandstand is full to bursting. The snowflakes disappear the instant they touch the canal's surface which is so smooth it might have been paved with graphite. The sculls are in the water. The two of them. Harold's and Percy Vinegar's.

"Harold puts the horn of hair into his craft and takes his place. The snow is falling so hard he can barely see the grandstand. It dampens the noise of the crowd so that he can hear the water dripping off the end of his oars. He is concentrating on his starting cadence which must not be too fast."

"Hatchman-Hatchman-Harold-*Hatch*man." Vardemaens is chanting, he has been doing so for some time, trying to convince Harold himself to join in.

Hatchman mumbles inaudibly. It may be "eighteen-eighteen-nineteen-*eight*een," he mumbles. Vardemaens persists, aspirating the syllables heavily, waving his arms in front of Harold as though he were leading a children's choir.

"HAtchman-HAtchman-HArold-*HAtch*man," intones Hatchman in his big, black voice. Vardemaens lets out a whoop, launches his glass towards the ceiling.

"It is the Household Cup," calls out John the nephew. "It is Percy Vinegar versus Harold Hatchman for the Household Cup. Everyone is there. Everyone. Harold is short an armful of blood. Snowflakes fall one by one on the back of his neck. The report of the starting gun is so deadened by the snow that he is not aware for an instant that the race has begun. He is surprised, caught short, he starts in at thirty-three, at least thirty-three. It is too fast. But even at thirty-three he can not keep up with Vinegar. He is not moving enough water."

Hatchman and Vardemaens are standing grand and vociferating:

"Hatchman-Hatchman-Harold-*Hatch*man."

"No, no," says John the nephew.

"Hatchman-Hatchman-Harold-*Hatch*man."

"No, no," he says. "It is no contest. Hatchman is two lengths behind. Better than two lengths. Vinegar could drop his oars and still win. It's all over."

"But wait!" says Vardemaens. "Look, Harold, look, look, look!"

"Yes," says Hatchman. "Look."

"It cannot be," says Vardemaens.

"Yes it can!" says John the nephew. "It's Vinegar, he *has* dropped an oar! He's off course and losing speed. Oohh, he's so flustered he's dropped it again! Hatchman's coming on. He's coming on. He's doing forty or I'm a deadman. He's going to go by him! It is not possible! It is not possible! Harold Hatchman is going to win the Household Cup!"

There is no end to it:

The swan-necked water spouts are trumpeting victory, the creamy porcelain is oinking joy. Harold Hatchman. The *barquettes*, terrines, wainscotting and florentines, Vardemaens' zinc-black enamel hair, the dented doorknob, and, above all, Hatchman himself, all of them are anthemizing without end: "Hatchman-Hatchman-Harold-*Hatch*man."

Some time later, Hatchman stepped over the last of the fading applause towards John the nephew, studied him closely, and said: "Would you like a haircut?"

"Ah," said Vardemaens, holding his breath.

John the nephew could not help shuddering at the liquid disconsolateness of Hatchman's eyes. Clearly, he thought, an orangutan would turn into a man if only it could remember last week's tree.

"It is an hour later," said John the nephew. "An hour later. They had had to rush Harold to the hospital. It was he who needed the transfusion now."

Hatchman slid his thick fingers into the scissors.

"Pamela Vinegar was still there," said John the nephew.

Slowly, as though he were working under water, Hatchman took up a snatch of hair and snipped off the ends.

"She was getting ready to leave," said John the nephew. "'I've got your hair,' said Harold. 'It's in my scull.'

"'Drink up,' said Pamela, nodding at the intravenous. 'Your brain is still a little dry.'"

The scissors sniggered in Hatchman's hand.

"'So you beat Percy,' she said. 'I was hoping you would. I'm pissed off at you now, though.'

"'I realize you're related to him,' said Harold.

"'Sure we're related. He's a jerk. So am I. I'd love to beat him at something. Tell me what it's like to beat Percy Vinegar at something. That one gorgeous, stomach-turning moment when it's I-win-Percy-you-lose. Tell me.'

"'I don't know,' said Harold. 'I passed out.'

"'You don't remember!' said Pamela.

"'No,' said Harold, 'I don't.'

"'He doesn't remember,' she said. 'Whew. Maybe one day, Harold, I'll be related to you. See you.'"

John the nephew looked at Hatchman standing behind him in the mirror. He saw a man made of mud. In his hand there was a grackle with a long beak made of metal. The grackle pecked gingerly at the new fruit of John the nephew's head. The man made of mud was uncurious, unamused by the liveliness of the bird.

"No, Pamela," said Vardemaens. "You'll never be related to Harold."

The barber shop was darker, smaller, it smelled of damp wood, of mould, the mirrors were milky and specked, a pair of silverfish conversed quietly as they climbed out of a sink.

The red chair was sticky and hard now. John the nephew watched Hatchman behind him in the mirror and saw that the man made of mud was drying out. He was suddenly afraid. The grackle dithered greedily. It stabbed off John the nephew's hairs and gulped them down. The man made of mud was drying out, taking form, turning into a barber, fat with the smell of emollients and oils, smelling the blood of John the nephew's head. The mud was melting onto the floor. He watched in the mirror as Hatchman squeezed the grackle brutishly, crushed its pumping lungs, raised it high over his head, the metal beak pointed hard at John the nephew's head. He was terrified. He covered his head with his arms as the scissors drove into his ear.

"John!" sang out Vardemaens' several voices, "I knew it would do him good!"

The scissors dug again into his ear, his blood flowed onto the red chair which had turned liquid under him, he slid down the liquid onto the floor, the red chair streamed over his ear, spreading out into the melting mud and easing under the door.

"John!" sang out Vardemaens again. "You're not supposed to fall right out of the chair, you know. You haven't hurt yourself have you?"

He wrapped his arms around John the nephew and drew him to his feet.

"I must have fallen asleep," said John the nephew.

"You wouldn't be the first," said Vardemaens. "Not the first by a long shot. Air is what you need."

John the nephew thought he might well fall asleep again. He felt as though he were standing in a layer of foam. Relief poured over him. He had not been discovered after all. Simply contaminated by his own imagination. The barber shop still smelled of tarragon and cheese. The Household Cup still stood on the table amid the dirty plates and empty bottles.

"Hungry Harold?" said Vardemaens.

"Not too," said Hatchman.

"You, John?"

"No sir."

He would be John Hatchman for the rest of his life if need be.

"Air," said Vardemaens, "is what we need."

And so out they went into the street where the sun shone whitely. The street was higher, harder, the facing walls were distant and crisp.

They walked for a time.

"The strap!" said Hatchman suddenly.

"Ayee," said Vardemaens, "I forgot the strap."

"The strap?" said John the nephew.

"We tie a strap between us when we go out. Harold wouldn't be able to find his way home if we were to get separated."

"I can go get it for you."

"Good enough. It's on a hook by the door. Here, take the key."

But the strap was not on a hook by the door. John the nephew looked desperately, his face hot with an apprehension he thought was merely a desire to not fail this first commission. He looked and looked but he could not find the strap. He had given up and was leaving when he spied it on the floor, partially hidden by the door itself. He picked up the strap and started running, filled with the strange conviction that he would not now be able to find Harold and Vardemaens. He told himself that it was his imagination acting up again, that they could not be far. He ran, looking down every side street and alley. He ran.

And soon enough he saw them, arm in bulky arm, the back of Harold's undershirt as broad as a skysail. He ran until he could see the ridges in Vardemaens' hair.

There is no hurry, he thought. I will be John Hatchman for the rest of my life.

He basked in the pure pleasure of knowing he could catch up to them whenever he wanted.

He was aware of a voice calling.

"John!" it called. "John Hatchman." His heart froze as he turned around.

"Hi!" she said. It is not possible, he thought. She appeared convivial, corn-fed. She was wearing a green hat pulled down over her forehead.

"The hat's a mite big, ain't it," she said. She tipped it up so he could see the bandage on her forehead. "That's what I get for leaning out of trains to shout at deaf people."

Her laugh beat softly on his chest.

"So," she said, "what brings you to this weck of the noods?"

"Oh, I've got an uncle with a barber shop not too far from here."

"Which explains the nifty new haircut," she said, smoothing his hair with her thumb. "Very nice."

She was wearing a coat made of curly black fur, holding it closed tightly at the throat. A bare knee broke through from time to time. She talked easily. Her yellow teeth were like smooth chips of wood.

"Well, John," she said soon enough, "I'm off I guess. Drop over. Any time. Just don't bring those sour-cream-and-onion condoms with you, eh."

"What sour-cream-and-onion condoms!"

"Oh that wasn't you? Must have been Dave the Rave. See you."

Her laughter continued to beat on his chest as he watched her recede. He knew there was now no point in running after Hatchman and Vardemaens. They would not be there. They would not. The sun shone whitely. He touched his ear. He wished it were bleeding. He wanted to yell at them that he was, he really was John Hatchman, before they forgot him altogether. He ran after them. He ran and ran. But they were not there.

NAMING DARKNESS

Daphne MacMillan, twenty-one, Associate of the Royal Conservatory of Music of Toronto, opened her front door to the mother and daughter standing on her doorstep, their backs to the late, warm, September sun. The mother held her daughter closely by the elbow, and regarded Daphne with a steadiness that indicated a desire to look away.

The daughter stood perfectly still. She possessed an air of self-containment which, in a fourteen-year-old, gives an impression of brilliance. She was dressed in a simple blue seersucker dress and white oxfords, a little too perfect and young, her brown hair very shiny and parted at the side. The sunlight shone through the rim of one of her ears, making it glow.

A lovely-girl, certainly. But she did not possess the crackling, pale eyes of a lovely-girl. She had no living eyes at all.

Instead, two black wounded slits set her face into a crude and constant squint.

"This is Janice," said the mother. "Janice has been blind since the age of two – she'll be fourteen in December, won't she. Janice thinks she would like to learn to play the guitar."

The two sat opposite each other on cold folding chairs in the small music room that smelled heavily of carpet. The notes spun out of Janice's guitar like pieces of ice. She made a mistake, the notes turned into stones. She bit into her German spice cookie and began again.

They were not always German spice cookies. They were sometimes ginger creams, or peanut crisps, or chocolate crinkles, or snickerdoodles. Daphne made them.

She listened spellbound, Daphne did, to her new student who had already made such astonishing progress. The speed and clarity with which Janice executed her technical exercises inspired Daphne with a fear that entered her through her own fingers, a fear that was unquestionably a form of joy.

The doorbell rang.

"That'll be your mother," said Daphne, putting Janice's guitar into its case and the case into Janice's hand, licking a corner of her sleeve and wiping away the crumbs from around Janice's mouth.

"Is she making any progress?" asked Janice's mother.

"She's a monster," said Daphne.

"That, I hope, means she's doing well," said Janice's mother.

"Very," said Daphne.

The mother took her daughter by the elbow, looked at her with suspicion.

"Have you been eating something?" she asked.

"No!" said Janice.

Daphne had considerable difficulty in referring to the classical composers for the guitar by their actual names. Sor became "Sorehead", Carcassi "Carcass", Aguado "O-god-no".

Janice had little trouble playing the music of these fussy and dusty Latins once she had learned it.

But learning it was painfully laborious. She was obliged to memorize the music at the very outset. To memorize it physically, in her hands. Daphne taught her note by note, beat by beat, placing Janice's fingers on the fingerboard and indicating which strings to strike. Entire lessons were devoted to a very few bars, mere seconds of actual playing time. Music which had been learned one week had inevitably to be relearned in subsequent weeks.

Daphne could at least allow herself the luxury of letting her tears flow quietly, provided she did not sniffle, or let her voice waver.

Janice, for her part, when her frustration became severe, turned very white and spat viciously, after which she remained so still she seemed to tremble.

As a result, Daphne began calling her "Moby Dick".

Recital rehearsal. Janice performed the 18th Sorehead study perfectly. The other students, who were crammed into Daphne's living room, applauded furiously. Particularly Chris.

The rehearsal over, and the living room filled to bursting

with rapid clouds of chatter, Chris looked for Janice, brushing the hair away from his forehead very intellectually with the heel of his hand.

"Chil*dren*!" said Daphne. The clouds thinned. She regarded the unsettled sky of her silent students regarding her.

"Well that was rather painful. I remind you that the real recital is *next* Saturday, so you still have time to sign up for piano lessons somewhere. Or tuba or even youka*lay*lee lessons."

Puffy, altocumulus laughter.

"But now it's time to *eat*. So if you'll direct your attention to the kitchen door, Moby has something to tell you."

Janice stood close to the doorframe, her excited smile and clumsy squint making her appear oafish and bright.

"Ladies and gentlemen," she said, "come to supper. Baked beans, and bread, and very good butter."

"*And*," said Daphne loudly into the cumulonimbus commotion of chairs, and standing up, and clapping, "Moby prepared everything herself."

"I know why you made beans," said Chris.

"Why?" said Janice.

"They're the musical fruit."

"The musical fruit?"

"Beans, beans the musical fruit. The more you eat the more you toot."

"The more you toot?"

"Fart," whispered Chris into her ear.

Janice laughed outright and turned her face in the direction of Chris's voice.

He did not leave her after that. Not for two seconds. He was full of clever things to say. Such as: "God your tone is clear. You don't play a note, you etch it. I mean me, sometimes I think I've got like fur-bearing fingers."

And then the other students had gone home and it was time to clean up.

"Want a hand?" said Chris loosely.

"No no no no no no no," said Janice.

So Chris, ostensibly just watching, very silently moved the dishes so that Janice could find them more easily.

"Don't do that," she said very softly.

"What was that?" said Chris. "Did you break out into idle conversation?"

But she did not repeat herself.

And then Daphne, folding chairs under each arm, backed into the kitchen and leaned against the counter beside Janice to rest.

"Have you got any muscles at all, Chris?" she said.

But when he made a move to help her, she glanced at Janice and reconsidered.

"No no, forget it. They're not heavy really. Your beans were a big hit, Moby."

And then Janice stepped on Daphne's foot with such violence that Daphne cried out, letting go the chairs which banged against her ankles. She clattered to the floor, sobbing.

"You know, Daphne," said Janice, adding water a tablespoon at a time to her pastry dough, "my darkness is not always the same. Sometimes it has a rhythm to it, sometimes it is very smooth, sometimes it makes a rustling sound like paper. And sometimes even it seems to be on the verge of disappearing. When I was young I used to give names to my darkness. My darknesses. I still do sometimes."

"Really," said Daphne, interested, but too occupied melting chocolate to notice that Janice had reddened. "What kind of names?"

"Oh, I don't know."

"Well, right now," said Daphne, observing her chocolate closely because it was getting very warm, "what kind of name would you give to your darkness?"

"I don't know. Domesticity."

"Really," said Daphne, looking up. She knew that Janice wanted her to like the name, and she wished she had been listening more closely. Perhaps then she would not have been so puzzled by it. So disappointed.

"She is lovely," said Percy Jones to Daphne amid the convivial din. They were watching Janice pose for the photographer. She was wearing the silvery full-length gown that Daphne had spent several hours altering. The blue ribbon and fat yellow medal hung crudely against the whiteness of her throat.

"She's a handful," said Daphne.

"Mmmnn," said Percy Jones.

"Down boy," said Daphne with an effusiveness brought out by champagne and the fact that she did not know Percy Jones. She was aware that, apart from being well over fifty, he was an organist.

"I've hardly slept all week. Between getting her fed and

watered and dressed and on time and warmed up. And massaged. She can't play without having half her body massaged. I still can't believe she's won. I've been a basket-case ever since the semi-finals. I get so effing nervous. *She's* been as cool as a cuke marching uphill in January but you know what? She hasn't really been playing as well as she can. Not really."

"I admire your devotion," said Percy Jones, turning towards Daphne. "I've been teaching for God knows how long. I've had good students of course, but never one with . . . the spark. Never one even with the promise of becoming a better organist than I am. If I were to get one now, I really wonder if I'd have the energy to . . . well, to do what you've done with Janice. The patience, the encour. . . ."

"Where is she?" said Daphne.

Janice was nowhere to be seen. Daphne hurried over to the photographer who was now taking pictures of the runners-up. He indicated the washroom.

There was a white-gloved woman wearing earrings as big as mints posted outside the washroom door.

"She asked me to bring her," said the woman. "She said she would be all right by herself inside."

"Thanks," said Daphne, going in.

Janice was supporting herself against a sink.

"Sorry. I lost track of you," said Daphne. "*Mille pardons*. Are you all done? I was listening to this somewhat slithery but otherwise quite hunkish old organist sing your praises and I just sort of. . . ."

"Get out of my *sight*," hissed Janice.

And then she laughed tightly at her little piece of cleverness.

Hockey. They loved to listen to hockey on television, Janice constantly trying to sooth Daphne's aggressive deriding of even their favourite players. She had a remarkable memory, Janice did, for hockey players' names and statistics. She also had an excellent memory for hockey gossip – which players were still available, which players had gone to jail for being with underage girls, which players were sleeping with which players' wives and so on – but her information was spurious, invented by Daphne as she read, supposedly, from the sports pages.

Camden, New Hampshire. The White Mountain Motel. Janice, in her excitement to put on her newly-acquired extra large T-shirt, banged her elbow against a lamp bolted to the floor.

"Ooooo," she moaned, finding a bed and lying down on it. "Pain o pain o pain."

"Daphne," she said after her elbow had cooled, "I've never been so ex*haus*ted in all my life. Never. Not *ev*er."

Her head was waggling and her gaping mouth made her nose wrinkle. Daphne had never seen her so extravagantly happy.

"Tell me, Moby, what name would you give to your darkness right now?" she said.

"You re*mem*ber," said Janice. "Mmm. Perseverance."

"And what's it like?"

"Oh, I don't know. It's *tired*."

And again Daphne was disappointed. She regretted having asked about this naming darkness, and she resolved not to ask again.

Janice was fingering the vinyl letters printed onto her T-shirt.

"They feel like dried mud," she said. "This . . . Body . . . Climbed . . . Mount Washington."

The Prelude in D minor, Fugue in A minor. The waiting darkness was breathing and hot in Redpath Hall. Janice had started in playing a little too fast. She was struggling against the guitar. The back of her neck was tense, her left thumb was aching, perspiration crawled down her armpit.

The darkness, sensing her vulnerability, began quickly to invade her, pushing its way silently into her mouth and ears and up her nose.

Until there was silence everywhere. Her hands and memory, the air, the audience, all were silent. She had stopped playing. She was lost.

"There's so much music to learn," said Janice in response to the interviewer's question. "A blind person, you see, has to remember it all, all the time, doesn't he. He has to rehearse everything continually in order not to forget. But there's so much music. So much. Really. So much. It's not possible. Do you think?"

"I'm sure I don't know," said the interviewer gently. "But teaching, you enjoy teaching do you?"

"Oh, I love teaching," said Janice.

Java. Swarms of Indonesians with dreamy eyes and small, pointless smiles. Lean, accommodating, smooth-faced insects.

The two traveled every summer now, becoming more adventurous with each season. They had many students between them, although Daphne taught far more than half.

And now they were listening to their guide in the pink-floored and poorly-lit hall which shuddered with the moaning of elderly men huddled at the far end, praying. The air was hot and moist and smelled of breathing animals. Black moss outlined the glimmering blue tiles that covered the walls. The guide was explaining to them the use of the *kukuri*.

"As you see," he was saying, "the *kukuri* is a sort of brush, the hairs are quite long and extracted from the tail of the buffalo and the handle too is very often made from the horn of the buffalo. The old men strike themselves in the face," he said, using rapid flicks of the wrist to make the tips of the hairs of the *kukuri* grate lightly across first one cheek, and then the other. "This they are doing for some time after which they are in a sort of trance, you see, they are still doing everything as they should be but they do not feel pain. And so they choose this moment to light the *soaka* which is a lamp but very very bright, a quite, quite bright lamp. They look very hard at the *soaka*, you see, for some minutes, and then they are blind."

"Fascinating," said Janice.

"And are all these men blind?" asked Daphne, moved by a need to hear her own voice.

"They have all used the *kukuri*, yes," said the guide. "When they are old. It is a very great honour, you see. To use the eyes to observe only the inner person."

"And how long," said Janice, "must they flick themselves in the face with the buffalo-hair brush before entering into this trance-like state?"

"Oh, not so many hours, yes," said the guide. "Not so many."

"Really," said Janice. The eagerness of her manner appalled Daphne who felt repulsed by the exotic masochism of the ritual, the animal odour in the monastery, and the bobbing intonation of the guide's voice.

"Could you," asked Janice, "light the soaka for me? I cannot help thinking I might perhaps be able to see it."

"Oh, I could yes," said the guide, "because you are so blind. But you, misses," indicating Daphne, "must put your hands on top of your eyes."

The soaka burst into light, extremely white and intense, and died almost immediately. Daphne, peeking between her fingers, had to turn her head away sharply.

"What's in it that burns so brightly?" she asked.

"It is this white powders, you see, which we in Indonesian are calling 'tears of the leopard.' This is a very old name and not very true. Quite fanciful I think. And you, misses, did you see the *soaka*?"

"I am not sure," said Janice, extremely agitated. "I think I may have. Would it be possible to taste a bit of the powder?"

"Oh Janice, really!" said Daphne.

"Yes," said the guide, "yes yes." He licked his finger, poked it into the lamp, and when he brought it out, the white powder clung to its tip. "A little," he said. "On the tongue. So."

Daphne could not help but watch as the guide touched his finger to Janice's blind, protruding tongue.

"You may swallow so little," he said. "Because you are so blind. You will understand better the *soaka*."

"You see," went on the guide, "the blindness of the *soaka* is not your blindness. It is a blindness of much light, not little. You, I think, live in the darkness."

"You, I think, talk too much," said Daphne.

"No," said Janice, a smooth and dreamy-eyed expression on her eyeless face, "it's fascinating. Really. Go on. Please."

"But that is all now," said the guide, smiling. "And so we go out."

All her life, Janice had difficulty releasing gas, a difficulty which became more acute as she grew older. So that by the time she had reached her middle thirties, she was susceptible to paralyzing cramps. To relieve this condition, it became necessary for Daphne to massage her abdomen every evening.

It did not matter whether Daphne were very tired, or feeling ill, she could not escape these sessions which, in general, were conducted in a silence broken only by a certain amount of internal gurgling and the soft flutter of air being released into the atmosphere.

Sometimes, though, they timed Janice's farts by solmization. As soon as they heard the characteristic hiss, they began singing "do, re, mi, fa," etc., stopping when the hiss died out. Even a short fart lasted at least an octave and some were so long that Daphne could not sing high enough and was left breathlessly mouthing the last syllables.

Nevertheless, Daphne was alarmed at how dry Janice was becoming. Her body seemed to be shrinking inside the loose skin. The numerous dark moles looked to Daphne like the heads of tacks holding the skin to the bone. The skin itself came away in flakes under Daphne's hands so that she took to dribbling baby oil along the small of Janice's bumpy spine and onto her midriff, and this made Janice shiver and squeal with anger.

Dear Miss McMillan,

My son Donald has been taking guitar lessons from your associate, Miss Janice Kaas, for over two years now. Today, when he arrived home from his lesson, I noticed that his ear was bleeding. When questioned about this, he told me that Miss Kaas attaches clothes-pegs to his ears and pulls on them every time he makes a mistake. I examined his ears and found them to be swollen and calloused. I cannot tell you, Miss McMillan, how offensive it is to me that such methods are employed in this day and age. In view of Miss Kaas's condition, I will not pursue this matter further, but I can assure you that my son will never again set foot . . .

A live radio programme. Janice was talking with the host in the cork-lined studio while Daphne listened outside on a monitor. Janice had been invited to appear on the show inasmuch as she was blind, had very nearly become a concert guitarist, and was now a highly-regarded teacher. She was saying that she had no regrets although she had had to live alone, with Daphne McMillan of course, but essentially alone, and that she had not been able to participate in the world of men and done all the things that that would have allowed her to do, although of course she could have if she'd really wanted to perhaps but it was so very much more difficult for the visually impaired wasn't it, but still she was proud of her accomplishments and so on. And then she was going on to say that she did regret one thing, she would have so much liked to have had children, a woman who had not had children could not consider herself truly fulfilled, and it was at this point that Daphne stormed into the studio and spat, "You ungrateful bitch!" before the host had time to put his hand over the microphone.

Janice had stopped eating. She did not even have the energy to use her blindness to defy Daphne. It was as if her darkness had turned into a pink-scented fog that neither interested nor displeased her.

Daphne would lie for hours in the upper berth of the heavy bunk beds they had bought years before when they had moved into their duplex – because the bedrooms were too small for two beds and because Janice could not fall asleep alone – and listen in vain for the familiar snortings and squeals, the kickings and brief cries of a life straining against sleep. They did not come. Janice slept peaceably on, exhaling with relentless precision as the large red numbers of the clock-radio silently changed.

So Daphne went to a grocery store and bought every bag of marshmallows, and on bath night, she emptied them all into the bathtub.

And when Janice came into the bathroom holding the Royal Doulton back-scrubbing brush she had purchased in a luxury boutique in Manchester, she asked:

"Have you run the bath?"

"Of course I have," said Daphne.

"It doesn't smell like it."

Daphne took her by the free hand and led her to the bathtub. "Foot up."

"Are you sure?" said Janice.

"Foot up," said Daphne.

Janice had lifted her leg over the edge of the tub when she became alarmed.

"No no no," she said. She tried to pull her leg out, but in so doing lost her balance and instead plunged her foot deep into the marshmallows. She screamed, wildly swinging the heavy china brush which rattled against the tiles, beat into the plastic curtain, and clipped Daphne on the nose.

Howling, Daphne took hold of Janice by the waist and down they fell into the bathtub, Daphne yelling that it was just marshmallows, marshmallows, marshmallows, just a joke, a j, o, k, e, until Janice sat in an awkward slouch against the taps, shivering with bleak, little sobs.

Daphne, blood still dripping from the tip of her nose, her face and scalp throbbing, regarded Janice, saw the jumble of her bones in the sunless skin, saw the small, pointless breasts, the crinkled face glazed with tears. A dying bird to be scooped up by any child, and thrown away with excited disgust.

"What did you do that for?" whimpered Janice.

"I don't know," said Daphne. "You *love* marshmallows."

"You can't stand to be left out, can you," muttered Janice.

"What?" said Daphne.

But Janice kept quiet. And then she picked up a marshmallow and started to nibble on it.

"It tastes like blood," she said.

"Yes, well, you kind of clobbered me with your brush. I've leaked several nosefuls all over your nice white marshmallows. They're all kind of pink."

Janice attempted unskillfully to spit out the marshmallow. It dribbled down her chin, which she wiped quickly with her hand.

Daphne got up out of the bathtub.

"Where are you going?" said Janice.

"Fishing," said Daphne.

"I want you to get me out now," said Janice.

"Go stew," said Daphne.

"I don't know what pink means," said Janice. "I don't want to stay here."

"Stew in my blood a while anyway," said Daphne, rejoicing.

"Well, what did I do," said Daphne in response to the interviewer's question. "I stared. I just stared. I did that for about seven months and then I took up smoking. Which was very stupid because now I can't stop. And after that, well I started playing the guitar again. I had been teaching all the time of course, when Moby was alive I mean, but I hadn't been playing very much. Moby was a terrible snob you know. She would never play duets with me. She couldn't even stand to hear me practice. If I wanted to get in an hour or two, I had to get up in the middle of the night, go down to the basement, and close myself in the bathroom. It's true.

But she had a right to be a snob. She was an absolutely brilliant guitarist as you well know. She didn't play a note, she etched it. She would undoubtedly have had an international career had it not been for her memory problems. But I mean, why should she get up in front of a bunch of people just waiting for her to suffer a memory lapse so they could say aahhhhh the poor thing, the poor poor thing, the poor poor thing thing."

"Yes. But *you* have an international career now."

"Let's not go diving off the shark-infested deep-end. On my last tour of England I gave mostly noon-hour concerts for little old ladies like myself. Except that I'm not so little anymore."

"But you've also done the U.S. And Germany. And your Villa-Lobos disc is highly acclaimed. Many people feel its among the best recordings made in Canada this year."

"Many people are very nice."

"And how do you explain that a snow-bound Canadian sensibility can so well enter into the rich Brazilian rhythms of Villa-Lobos?"

"Well now, that *is* a lot of balls. Really. Villa-Lowblows is a wonderful wonderful composer. Despite his smelly cigars. I just let him take my hand and try to keep up with him."

Daphne MacMillan, sixty-two, Professor of Music, sat in her, as she called it, bite-sized condominium that smelled heavily of the same carpet that had lain in her music room for many years.

She thought how curious it was that her resolve was so firm, considering that until short minutes ago, she had not once thought of doing what she was about to do. And yet it was so simple and obvious, like the explanation to any good trick.

But it was important to her to have a name. Not crucial. Impermanence would do perhaps. Impermanence. Imperm. Anence.

Janice, Janice, Janice. Beautiful and overblown to the bitter end.

It was odd. She had always thought she would become reflective in her old age. She had always thought old people were reflective. But most of the time there wasn't much of anything going on inside her head.

Years went by as quickly as months had used to. At this rate, she thought, she would be seventy by September.

So it did not matter if her life had been wasted. Because it had now been lived. Life *is* a sort of trick, she thought. Once it's over you're left wondering how it was done. A good trick. Not good good. Good effective.

Impermanence. A musical name at least.

Janice, Janice. Dead at forty-two. A dry white slouch with a bowel full of driving cancer cells. Diagnosed and dead all in a week.

My darkness is not always the same, she thought. She could easily smell the chocolate warming. Sometimes it is very smooth. Sometimes it rustles. Sometimes it seems on the verge of disappearing. A trick of the memory.

No. She did not like impermanence.

It was Janice's name, not Daphne's. And Daphne had, as it were, figured out how her trick was done.

There was a time, she thought, when she would have

been appalled at the idea that life was nothing but a trick. Those were the days of course when she worried that she wasn't eating in enough French restaurants and seeing enough Japanese films, not drinking strong enough coffee, not touching enough, not being touched enough. And here Daphne smiled. Those were the days when she read women's magazines by the handful in order to prove to herself that she wasn't living her life properly. And again, Daphne smiled with an eagerness that was unquestionably a form of joy. For in another region of her thinking, she had found her name, although she had not as yet admitted it to herself. There, she was remembering exactly where she had placed the can of beans, and the can-opener, the pot, the bread, and, of course, the butter, the butter. Her first meal in her new last life.

Those were the days, she thought, when she would have been revolted at the sight of her sixty-year-old self dropping cigarette ash onto her tweed suit, childless, loveless, clutching her little statuette for Best Classical Solo Recording by a Female Artist Living in a Pink Fog.

And so it was the appropriate moment to begin. She took up the *kukuri* that Janice had so insisted on buying – although they had not been for sale and she had only been allowed one because she was blind and, of course, willing to pay an arm and both legs – the *kukuri* that she had taken down from the china cabinet along with the *soaka*, and, holding the horn handle loosely, flicked her wrist rapidly so that the tips of the hairs of the *kukuri* grated lightly across her cheek.

Janice, Janice, Janice. Naming her darkness for the last time. With her dead eyes and her fetid breath. I can see it growing inside me, Daphne. It beats like a heart. It is my darkness and its name is faithlessness. Its name is impermanence.

Janice, Janice, Janice, thought Daphne. Beautiful and overblown to the bitter end.

Janice, she said. I do not understand your names. They're weird polysyllabic names I think. Heartless. They're too much like you.

And here, Daphne flicked her wrist again so that the *kukuri* grated across her other cheek. She was terribly excited.

Listen Moby, she said. I have figured out how all my tricks are done, so to speak. And you, poor thing, never saw how any of yours were done. And again, she flicked the *kukuri*. I have my name. Not that it matters because you won't like my name. And anyway my darkness will really be a lightness won't it. Again flicking the *kukuri*. But I might as well tell you its name will be very good butter. Do you like it? Again, flicking. Very good butter. No, well I told you you wouldn't. And again, flicking. But wait for me, Moby. I'll be along before too many moons have passed and we can play some of those Emilio Poo-hole duets. And again. The duets you wished you could find a partner for and afterwards you can give *me* the back-rub for once. And again. And we can dream up names together till the cows come over the hill, over and over the hill, again and again. And again.

In Memoriam P.H.

"PETER," SAID THE BIRD

Peter awoke in a high state of excitement that was either a considerable happiness, or an acute fear. He remembered a hot and unpleasant dream in which an unlit room with sharp corners turned and twisted inside his chest. He remembered this dream because now, despite his alertness and despite the wet noise of the February night outside, the dream persisted, softened. It was an open room that was inside his chest now, with summer windows, with glass curtains that luffed inward occasionally as though barely awake, and with small birds darting in and out so suddenly that Peter could not catch sight of them, and this made him want to laugh.

He heard, in the bed beside him, his wife's breath whistling in her nose, and a squadron of red and sentimental birds flew into the room and landed on the floor in his chest. With each breath, the birds flew up into the room. The air whistled in their wings.

Five.

Peter was fat. He was. So too was his wife. Her hands and her mouth were fat. She was in, moreover, a fat mood, having spent the last four days in the same sleeveless pyjamas, never going out and eating nothing but olives and melba toast, until she was caked with the smell of vinegar and perspiration.

He was very agitated. He saw himself again with his foot in the empty beer case, Richard Fitzgibbon taking him by the shoulders, and the soft voice that boomed. He could not understand why he continued to dream even though he was awake. Because he had only five days left. Yes, but it was not this that frightened him. It was the fact that he could not catch sight of the birds, so rapidly they flew into and out of the room in his chest.

He remembered his wife as she had sat earlier beside him on the sofa watching the French channel because, as she had said, she felt like feeling stupid. In the dark living room with nothing but the nervous blue light of the television turning her skin gray and the shadow of her nose, and Peter who could see himself still wearing his winter coat, sitting sideways in order to look into the armholes of her pyjamas, watching as she got up to change channels, seeing for a moment against the television screen and through the lifeless cotton the silhouette of her pneumatic thighs and in flew the red birds again as big and barking as dogs so that Peter was sure that the cause of his excitement was living and intense.

Five days. There was still time. There was.

His wife's body sleeping and whistling in the bed beside him gave off so much heat that Peter had to move away from her. There were no cigarettes in the bedroom, and the glass curtains in the room in his chest were moved by complicated breezes.

And again he remembered, saw himself stumbling on the low step that led into the sunporch, grabbing the white wicker plant hanger to steady himself, stepping erratically into the empty box of Golden Light beer.

"Whoooah," said Richard Fitzgibbon rushing up and taking him by the shoulders. "Steady, Pete."

And the soft voice that boomed.

There were birds and there was laughter everywhere, but there was not time. Not in five days.

The laughter rattled along the roof of the sunporch, but Peter could not laugh. His face was hot. The room was twisting inside his chest, making him shift his weight in order to accomodate it. His feet were trapped in the blankets and the birds in the room insisted on flying directly at him, staring at him with their one, oval eye.

There were no cigarettes in the bedroom and the birds flew at him with their one eye, winking infuriatingly the other, the withered eye. He could no longer bear the smell of perspiration and olives, above all he could not endure the heat of his wife's body beside him, squeezing itself around his stomach, pressing itself into the space between his lungs.

Suddenly and with surprising violence, his feet kicked at the clinching blankets. With such sudden violence in fact that Peter jerked over the edge of the mattress and fell heavily onto the floor, his legs still on the bed, his feet still caught up in the covers. The whistling in his wife's nose stumbled over itself briefly, and then resumed on a lower note.

The birds were gone. Peter felt much better.

He succeeded in disengaging himself and began feeling his way on all fours to the bathroom. He must, he thought, be getting a cold. Small wonder. Small wonder indeed, having already spent on this Sunday night an indeterminate period of time sleeping in the snow under a taxi. Not to mention diving into the mud at third base.

He remembered falling under the taxi. Not without pride. Having drunk too much beer, smoked too much dope, and breathed in too much black winter air. So that his drug-bitten and frosted brain had been no match for the icy sidewalk, and no sooner had he stepped out of the cab than down he went, slamming the door shut and falling under the car in a single move that no amount of sober practice could have perfected.

Imagining again the taxi-driver's horror as it must have been when, barely having started to pull away, he heard the scream coming from the area of his muffler, a scream so brief and that faded so suddenly into a thin, lifeless hum that he, the driver, must have been immediately convinced that the substantial body now lying under his car was either dead or dying quickly. Watching the stricken driver get out, glare with hatred at Peter's big body, seeing him haul Peter out with desperate strength, rush back into the car, grab the small cross made of reed that hung from his rear-view mirror, stuff it into one of Peter's coat pockets, and drive off madly into the swaying snow.

He had made his way now to the bathroom. The winter coat was where he had left it hanging on the hook inside the door. He found the pocket and the small cross made of reed that he would keep, he thought, for the rest of his life surely. He sat down backwards in the dark onto the toilet seat where he had been sitting perhaps no more than two hours earlier as he drank one last rye. The bottle was still on one side of the toilet, the bag of chocolate chips on the other, and the cigarettes, thanks be to the fantasy-dump, were taped to the back of the tank where his wife would not find them.

He remembered brilliantly the breathtaking sensation of the taxi's moving slowly over him, the terrifying pain above his ear, and the scream that hurled itself through his mouth like hot gold. But he had realized almost instantly that the pain was caused by nothing more than his hair being caught under one of the tires, the scream had turned into a wounded laugh even before it was spent, and Peter, exhausted by his own relief, had fallen fast asleep.

He blew smoke out into the dark bathroom, imagining it splashing against the mirror. He fingered the cross made of reed with amusement, and with pride. He would keep it for the rest of his life surely.

He did not know how long he had slept in the snow. A matter of minutes, no more. He remembered waking with a start, aware immediately of his surroundings, exaggeratedly sober, the lights around him piercing and precise. There had been a coolness in him and a desire to dance. He had entered the front door cleverly, soundlessly, to find his wife watching the French channel in the dark, had sat beside her in his coat, thankful there would be no need on this night to report in, to go through his wasted afternoon making a television commercial for a local carpet store, lip-syncing thirty-eight thousand times a song pre-recorded in San Diego, thankful he could dream in peace of sliding his hand into the armholes of her pyjamas.

Five days and only five.

"Not to mention," he said quickly out loud, knowing that he must continue to remember in order to keep the birds away. His voice broke noisily over the bathroom tiles, the relief of smoking made his eyes water. "Not to mention."

The softball game that had occupied his morning: with Sophia Cunfaloney pitching, her several sweaters tucked into her tights so that her hips appeared to be carved out of soap, wearing a first baseman's mitt that she had to keep taking off so she could lob the ball with her right hand, the ball that was painted red so it could be seen easily in the snow, and Peter swinging the bat with all his might naturally, hot spirits of pain biting him in the armpits, the ball on its way to the outfield, Peter praying someone would catch it but no, the ball clearing the many outfielders but not the fence, run Peter run, rounding second with all his might naturally, launching his many pounds head first into the third base mud, safe by a mile, wet to the soul, lighting a cigarette right there on third base in order to appease his bouncing heart and his angry body's need to vomit.

And again he saw himself stumble on the low step that led into Richard Fitzgibbon's sunporch, holding onto the wicker plant hanger, his foot stuck in the empty case of Golden Light beer.

A single brown bird flew into the room in his chest and observed Peter with curiosity, cocking its head in its particular way, as Peter heard again Walter Laking's soft voice that seemed to boom:

"Golden Lightfoot I presume."

The laughter rattled over the sunporch, Walter Laking emerged through it to shake Peter's hand, smiling with the warm-hearted diffidence of a man secure principally in his intelligence, and Peter, unable to laugh, his cheeks burning, so impressed he was by the cleverness of the remark and the resonant delicacy of the voice.

Not to mention, of course, Walter Laking's reputation as a man who had suffered long and rare diseases of the limbs, who washed his hair every day with beer, and who had written highly regarded poems and books.

Not to mention further that Richard Fitzgibbon had said on the phone that he, Walter Laking, expressly wanted to meet him, Peter McKim, he did not know why.

He sat in the dark bathroom and watched Walter Laking pass in front of him through the door that led from the sunporch into Richard Fitzgibbon's hallway, with the awkward stride of a big man on insufficient legs, a manner of walking that did not however make him look older than his fifty years, but younger. He might almost have been a boy of fourteen, eager, if not robust. So that Peter had felt a desire to put one arm behind Walter's knees, the other across his shoulders, and sweep him up into the air, a desire so strong in fact that he had had to turn to Denis Leblanc behind him and ask if he knew what Eskimos got from sitting too long in cold kayaks.

And there they sat, Richard and Denis and Peter and Walter and two or three others, talking around Richard's linoleum kitchen table, the new and as yet unvarnished cabinets smelling garishly of new hardwood, Walter's head framed by the windows over which wandered a number of fat and sluggish flies brought out by the exceptionally hot October sun, his beery hair standing straight up, and on his cheek a ripe, attentive pimple.

He sat in the dark on the toilet fingering the cross made of reed and thinking he must get out, he could barely breathe, and yet he could not prevent himself from hearing them talk over his head, Walter Laking taking on the Unitarian minister whose name was Rex, saying, "I grant you, Rex, that faith is one of the inspiring mysteries of life. But doubt is no less inspiring. Or mysterious. Your God is, finally, nothing but a place for us to dump our fantasies."

The room in his chest was bursting with birds no larger than bubbles, zillions of them rising, rising, making a watery sound very much like applause. God yes, he thought, God yes. Except that it was one Peter Pumpkin-eater who was the dump full of dreams, wasn't it. God yes, he thought, trying to convince himself that he did not hear something suspect in Walter's unrelenting cleverness. He heard Walter's voice wash over his head: "Who do I write for?" observing his fingers tracing patterns over the silver-flecked, black linoleum. "I don't know. I've often thought what I should do is write every book with a different pen name, and give every main character the name Walter Laking. I mean, I don't really know for whom I exist, do I?"

He could not stay in the bathroom, he could not breathe. He wanted to sweep Walter up into the air. He crawled out into the hallway.

"Peter," said Walter Laking, "I'm glad you came. I'd like to talk to you."

He propped himself against the wall in the unlit hallway.

"Peter," said Walter, "Rex here wants to do one of my children's plays next Easter in his church. Nothing too too awful . . . but it does need a lot of bodies, especially little ones. A hundred children say. Apart from the main cast."

"Peter," said the bird in the room in his chest who had been observing him all this time, his head cocked in his particular way.

"Peter," said Walter, "it's a sort of what, a happy thing. A folk-tale really. The children sing."

"Peter," said the bird. "Stop crying out loud."

"Peter," said Walter, "I realize you're a busy man. But we thought your radio show might be the ideal vehicle to, you know, round up a bunch of chilluns, promote the thing a little. We could do it through the schools if you've got too much on the go obviously, but . . . I mean every kid and his uncle knows you, Peter. And likes you."

"Peter," said the bird, "you know I really think you're quite the guy. You've got talent, you've got brains. I think you're just a piece of pie."

"What do you think?" said Walter. "Think you could recruit a hundred kids for me? Four months give you enough time?"

"*Four* months," said the bird. "Four *hun*dred maybe."

"Peter," said Walter, "I know you're very busy. I thought you might be interested."

"Peter," said the bird, "seriously, you're so bright and so aware. And so cleverly you manage your personal affairs."

"Well I'm glad then," said Walter.

"*But*," said the bird, "you might have at least *start*ed, you might have at least asked *some*body, you might have at least.

Four *months* the man gives you. Four months for his rinky-tink folk-tale. Of all the. Have you even *read* it? Five days left, five and only five, and you haven't even *read* the *play*. You haven't even *start*ed, you haven't . . ."

"Kiss off," said Peter. "Just kiss off. God you love to heckle. To flap your wings and scoff."

"Peter," said the bird. "Calm yourself. Stop crying for crying out loud. There's time, there's time." He continued to observe Peter with his head cocked in his particular way.

"Well I'm glad then," said Walter. "It'll be great to have a celebrity associated with the project."

"Peter," said the bird. "You want to do this for Walter, don't you?"

"God yes," said Peter. "God yes."

"You want to sweep him up into the air in your arms don't you?"

"Yes," said Peter.

"There's time," said the bird. "If you spend *all* day on the phone. Put it out on the air and you'll have *five* hundred kids in twenty minutes. There's time."

"There is," said Peter. "I know there is."

"Peter," said the bird, "don't make me laugh. Look at you. Look at yourself rounding second with all your might. Run Peter run. Diving head first into third base, mud up to your eye-balls. Don't make me laugh. Look at yourself lip-syncing "our prices will floor you" for the thirty-eight thousandth time. Peter Peter Peter. For crying out loud. Don't make me laugh. There isn't time. A hundred kids, Peter. A hundred. You haven't even *start*ed yet, you haven't even asked your *own* kids."

He was swaying down the hallway now, to the children's room.

"Peter," said the bird. "What's this ga-ga about the great Walter Laking anyway? Have you even heard from him since? He listens to the radio, you know. He knows you haven't done doodley. He's dumped you, Petie. Gone and got his own kids. He *knows* people, you know. He's liked. Look at the state you're in, and all for a sort of what, a happy thing. You're out of all proportion, Petie. Out of all. Between you and me, Petie, you're dreaming, you're making me laugh."

He opened the door to the children's bedroom and was groping for the light switch when down he went. The room in his chest was red and trembling now, with many flat-billed birds chewing at it awkwardly, stumbling over themselves, rubbing their eyes under their stubby wings.

"Peter," said the bird. "What were you dreaming about when you accepted? You couldn't have done it if you'd had five *hun*dred and five days. Am I right? I mean, you've got thirty-eight thousand things to do like eating chocolate chips and sleeping in the snow. Am I right? Walter Laking my withered eye. Tell me, try, who do you exist for anyway? For the love of Pete."

Suddenly and with surprising violence, the bedroom was filled with light, piercing and precise. Peter was immediately struck by how high the ceiling appeared when viewed from his position on the floor. In fact, the entire room seemed much larger than he remembered it. His lungs were already as stiff as hard new wood, and his failing heart tasted like a bad nut. So, he thought. He was intrigued by the fact that there was not really any pain that hurt. And yet surely, he thought, surely.

His wife, after all, her hand still on the light switch, was standing over him, fat with horror. And she was screaming, although Peter did not so much hear the scream as he saw it, hot and golden, streaming from her mouth. There was in the room as well another sound which was very much like applause, but which, as Peter realized, was the crying of the two children. So it must be so.

He was disappointed by the fear in his wife's face. It made his own fear rise. He could barely remember. No, nothing now. Not for the life of him. Nothing at all. All he could see was his wife's fear. And thereby his own, rising, rising, making a watery sound in the room in his chest.

His wife squatted beside him, her tears dripping onto his face. She tried to lift his head, but in so doing, lost her balance and fell onto him, so that he felt, through the lifeless cotton pyjamas, her nauseating heat. He realized then that his fear at least was living and intense. And Peter, exhausted by his own relief, fell fast, fast asleep.

THE WALNUT SHELL

Tired he was. And certain that he was forgetting something. Shoes, watch, gym pass. Something.

It was too dark and too warm for December. There were tufts of snow on the ground, like mildew. An unhealthy, spongy mist absorbed the greenish light drifting from the high band of windows in the new sports complex. The sports complex was so new, in fact, that it still sat amid the broken bricks and heavy scraps of paper, the odd pieces of wood and the small rubble of its own construction.

Too tired, he thought. Twenty-two quarter-mile repeats are too many. Many too many. Walking gingerly along the treacherous boards, trailing the laces of his winter boots, the tilting boards that led to the mud-lot where his car was parked. Counting haphazardly his steps: *twen*ty-and-a-*twen*ty-three-a-*twen*ty-and-a-four-and-a-five-and-a-*twen*ty. . . His sweat clothes packed under his arms, his sports bag in his teeth. Twenty-two quarter-mile repeats all under 64 seconds. Speed. Yes. You've got to have speed. Rubbing his pockets with his elbows, finding his wallet, hearing the jingle of his keys.

What, he thought, am I forgetting?

He had forgotten his gloves. He knew that. In the morning he had forgotten them. So now he had his hands pushed into the toes of his running shoes. Therefore it was not the running shoes that he had forgotten.

Forty-*three*-forty-*for*ty-forty-fifty-fifty-*one*-fifty . . .

Hey, hey, said Eric, twenty-two is a little much, isn't it?

Eric. Eric the Coach, he thought. Where have you got to?

You've got to have speed, said Eric, but the idea isn't.

I know, he thought, what the idea isn't.

There was, in the middle of the as-yet-unpaved parking lot, a temporary orange spot-light attached to the top of a pole so bent and knotted that it appeared unnatural, improper. It irritated him.

The idea is to pull your blood-sugar down, said Eric. Not.

Not to run yourself into exhaustion, he said.

He could not rid himself of the odour of the mid-green latex paint that coated the new concrete walls of the sports complex, or of the rhythmic din of the two huge air-exchangers in the gymnasium. Too tired he was. He walked off the end of the boardwalk into the gaum of the parking lot where his car looked to him like a deserted military vehicle, in part because its blue colour was turned to olive by the orange spotlight, in part because its tires were covered with mud.

Anda-five-*anda*-fix-*anda*-*anda*-*anda*-anda-*free*-anda-*four* . . .

Eric, Eric, Eric, he thought.

His beleaguered car was the last cold car left in the mire of what seemed to him a lost battlefield. The din in his ears might well have been that of distant engagements, or it might only have been the breathing of the soldier running beside him, the brush of his ammunition belt against his khaki fatigues.

Why, he had asked Eric, remembering how drained he had been, his hands on his knees, the saliva white and sticky in his mouth, why did I think there was someone running beside me?

No, said Eric, there was no one even close. You won by three seconds. At *least* three seconds.

Yes but I heard him breathing.

Thairty-*tooo*-thairty-*three*-thairty-*four* . . .

Who knows, said Eric, putting his hands on his own knees so he could look into his eyes. When you're running under pressure and deep in oxygen debt, you're at the very outer edge of experience, aren't you. The inner edge of dreaming. Use it. Run into it.

And still he had the impression of having forgotten something. Was he wounded in the shoulder? In the eyes? He curled his toes inside his unlaced boots so that he would not lose them in the heavy mud. Was this then the Italian front? The oppressive Neapolitan winter mist?

Tired he was. Too tired. Twenty-two repeats. His little military car remained as far off as ever, bobbing in front of his eyes in the orange air.

Is it Eric I am forgetting?

Thinking how they had never seen Eric like that. Had

never seen him splay himself out for all to see, rattling on behind a table full of empty glasses, with that ill and feverish look of a man not used to drinking. Eric the Coach, with his Irish accent, his vigourous black hair and his loose eyes, his eyes, yes, he thought, his eyes that gave the impression they might very well roll out of sight with one good jolt and yet that saw so well. For it had always been Eric who drove the Windstar from meet to meet, his hands glued to the wheel, and Eric who said despite the starless sky and the emptiness of the road that it would soon be raining, and Eric who, when asked how he could tell, answered that he could see it.

*Hun*erd-n-ten-*Hun*erd-n-levn . . .

Eric the Coach, Eric the Father, Eric the Holy Ghost.

He could see now the familiar pattern of rust spots below the keyhole of his car. He knew he would not now remember what it was he had forgotten and yet he could not keep himself from trying to remember, estimating there to be twenty-four steps still to his car, counting them down, the brushing of the ammunition belt still in his ears, and still listening as Eric said you're at the inner edge of dreaming aren't you, use it, run into it, and he straightening up so smartly that the crown of his head clipped Eric on the chin, three seconds he had won by, fifteen metres, and still he could distinctly hear the strained, relentless breathing of another runner off his right shoulder.

Twenty-two quarter-miles, he thought. All under 64 seconds. Much too much.

*Four*teen-*Thir*teen-*Twel*vah . . .

Love, said Eric, chattering away from behind another batch of empty bottles, his ill eyes darting, love tastes bad.

Swallow love and it eats you. It eats all your three ideas and your half-dozen possibilities. The love-eaters read magazines in grocery stores. They wave to each other in neighbourhoods and grow marigolds. They try to make real children, and all they make is more lovers.

And he, never having seen Eric like this, impressed, impatient, unable to respond, bristles of pain scampering like mice periodically up his left hamstring, worrying him.

The heartache and the thousand, said Eric, his forehead as though feverish. Nothing like it. Nothing like losing. I lose, you win. Looking at him with his sharp loose eyes, saying, Such solace really. Such queace and piet. Behold, a new man sits before you. A new man with his eyes bandaged up and just a bit of a peephole with a flap in the top of his head through which appears the little piece of ceiling or sky or whatever directly above. Lovely, really. Such calm. Losing, you see, brings you peace. It's winning keeps the soul writhing.

And he, not understanding, saying, Eric, Maureen and me . . .

At night, said Eric, I might see two or three stars at most through my little hole. And if I'm very lucky, none at all.

And he, not understanding, appalled, restless, anxious about his injured thigh, standing up to leave.

See you, said Eric. Keep winning, won't you?

He was sitting in his cold car now, looking out to where the beams of the headlights struck the evergreens that lined the parking lot. Beams, he thought. Joists of light. He had snapped them on because he could not see where to put the key into the ignition. The insides of his eyelids were very wet and he was annoyed that he had lost count of the last steps to his car.

Because he had not understood how tired he had been. Had not understood that he was leaving Eric for the last time, that he would never see him. Never.

Is that then what I'm forgetting? he thought.

Never again.

Eric the Coach. Eric the Friend. Eric the Overthrown.

Thinking, I did have friends. Millions of them. Friends who ran beside me, football friends and saxophone friends, friends who liked trig and friends who wanted to go to Burma, and friends who turned into girls who kissed forever with their hands on the back of my head, and then turned into friends again.

He was too tired to resist. Maureen was there, in her apartment, her flat as she called it, singing in the dead, summer light, singing in a shapeless voice that he might have imagined belonging to a wingless blue insect, unmoving, until she stepped idly in front of the nylon-curtained window, the glaring white light wrapping itself around her, leaving him to blink in the beating, hot shadows.

What's that you're singing? he said.

He was concentrating on the headlight beams because, whether due to the wetness of his eyes, or to the slinking mist, he had the impression that they were not flowing out of his car, but into it.

Rotterdam, the Calypso International at the . . . the *Leichtathletikpark?* The Athletic Park at any rate, where the shower stalls were old old, with swinging doors made of dark wood, and reeling steam that smelled of varnish and ammonia. He had floated down the streets of Rotterdam that night between Eric and Maureen, having died in the last hundred metres, his arms numb and his chest knotted, pleading with himself to relax and count, and count, and count, counting the strides through the last dying metres, three thousand two hundred and forty-six of them in all, twenty-two fewer than his previous best, and, incredibly, as he floated sleepily through the Rotterdam night on the arms of Eric and Maureen, no one, not anyone, had passed him, incredibly, for when he crossed the finish line he no longer even had the sensation of moving forward.

Until eventually they had found themselves in a huge barn-like club, sitting in the balcony, the dance floor below them, the waiter oriental, dressed in coveralls, shirtless, manic and perspiring, laughing with them as they laughed at his crippled English, shaking his tray with one hand as though it were warm and needed cooling, caressing his nipple with the other.

When who should appear on the stage below but, but David Bowie, yes David Bowie, in Rotterdam of all places, singing heeere am I sitting-in-a-tin-can, tall and white-faced, executing surprisingly shaky knee-bends and pirouettes, the microphone cord jumping with each movement, not of course because he was too old and too stoned, but because, as the three of them realized at the same moment, he was not David Bowie at all, but an impersonator.

And so it was either go down and dance or fall asleep at the table, and they had waded into the thick green pond of slowly swirling homosexuals, all of them naked to the waist, it being by now the hour for sad dances against the flesh of the night's new familiar, the impersonator having turned into Procol Harum, among others, and Maureen having slipped off their shirts and then slyly taken off her own white T-shirt. So they would not feel out of place.

They danced. The three of them. Incredibly. He had won the Calypso International. He was too tired to resist, and Eric had wrapped his arms around them, his white, freckled Irish arms, so they had danced, the three of them together, a motionless, deaf waltz, his body as though rocking gently, lapped by gay perfume, adrift on Maureen's briny skin.

What's that you're singing? he asked weakly in the dead summer light.

Nothing, she said. Something I wrote for you.

Alone in Saint-Cloud, sitting under the bridge with the Nigerian runner who was pouring as much sugar onto his hands as into his yogourt, where the colour of the limestone sand as the shadow of the bridge fell upon it was so exactly the tone of Maureen's slouching spine that he, when the Nigerian lazily carved a line through the sand with the edge of his sandal, had angrily slapped the yogourt out of his hand.

Something I wrote for you, she said. Nothing very . . .

Nothing. Very.

Beams, he thought. Joists of light.

Because he at least had been perfectly happy to be in the Santa Claus Parade. Feeling again how cold his feet had been, and the dizziness caused by the shuddering motion of the float on which he was standing sideways, the twin chrome exhaust pipes of the tractor blowing black lumps of smoke over the rolling artificial snow which was as hard as stone, and over the leafless skinny trees painted white. Oh there were football players on the float with their helmets, and tennis players with rackets, swimmers with flippers and so on, all of them a-waving. He was there for the Supernova Track Club with Jill Donohue, and with Eric.

And then there was the girl lying down, her figure skates hooked over her shoulder. He remembered being struck by her wrinkled tights which were more the colour of wood than of skin, by her hair which was partly black and partly white and very stiff under the marshmallow hat which had slipped off – startled, she had said, hadn't she, sitting in front of her mirror with the cards and notes stuck in the frame, in her red slip, and with the blue-lettered towel that she had stolen from the gym over her shoulders, the bottle in her hand, saying, This? This is called ice. It helps make my hair look . . . startled. I like that.

And he remembered being struck above all of course by the fact that, in the middle of the Santa Claus parade, she was sound asleep.

Startled, he thought. Feeling again the prickly quality of her hair against the palm of his hand, thinking it might well have been the fur of some ancient animal with a long snout.

You startle me, she had said. I like that, too.

And was the Santa Claus Parade the first time that Eric had seen her too? He did not know. It could not have been. It must have been. It must.

Eric, he thought. Eric. Such solace. It's winning keeps the soul wriggling.

There they were, Eric and Maureen, watching the steeple-chasers practise the water obstacle, careful not to touch, lovers certainly but only since the day before, or perhaps the day before that, and Eric saying enthusiastically, Watch them through half-closed eyes. The impression should be of a mingled mass of colours flowing across the barrier and skimming the water. A single, smooth, silky motion. It's the rhythm which must first be achieved. The rhythm. We'll address technical details later.

Eric the Palaverer. Eric the Coach. Eric the Brokenhearted.

You win, said Eric. I lose. Such calm really.

Something I wrote for you, said Maureen. Singing in the dead summer light in a tuneless voice that might have belonged to a blue oily beetle. Nothing very.

Sing it again, he said.

Was he wounded in the shoulder? In the eyes? He was stiff and cold now, his hands on the steering wheel were more the colour of wood than of skin, and his car was rushing swiftly backwards, sliding along the flowing headlight beams.

Three thousand two hundred and forty-six strides in all. Twenty-two fewer than his previous best. How many people, he thought, can count to a thousand on their fingers? Nine hundred and ninety, actually. And Eric never knew. Never knew about the endless stream of numbers clicking through his fingers. His longest run, twenty-one thousand four hundred and fifty-nine strides. His shortest, three hundred and eleven. And so on. And on and on.

You smell of blood, sang Maureen, wrapped in the dead light of the window. Of blood and of March.

Too tired he was. Too tired to resist.

April Fool's Day. Eric giving an armful of flowers to Maureen saying, not very April foolish I know, love kills the imagination I guess, and then turning to him, giving him the clothespin and a short speech: I watched a woman, the other day when it was so windy, dressed in a winter coat she was, leaning over the banister of her veranda hanging out sheets madly flapping away and I thought, now there he is, all his umpteen miles of training, his intervals, his wind-sprints, his knee-raisers, his stride-outs, all of it, everything, his whole life flapping away ready to surge off into the wind like those sheets. But for your Calypso run. And your other big races. You're a . . . winner, for lack of a better word. Remember that. That's your clothespeg.

And he, reaching into his pocket, knowing he should not, Eric still beaming about his flowers and his clothespin, giving the walnut shell to Maureen.

How *thought*ful, she laughed. *Just* what I. Oh, there's something inside is there.

The something falling to the floor as she separated the two halves of the shell.

Maureen bending to pick up the charm, for a charm it was, a gold charm of a runner, enclosing it in her hand, not looking at either of them.

It's alive, she said.

You smell of blood and of March, sang Maureen in the dead light, of wounds and healing wounds. His heart stammering in the irritating shadows. I see you spattered with joy, she sang in her oppressive, pretty way, you sparkle like topsoil, shine like mud.

The car flowing swiftly backwards through the unhealthy mist, the evergreens receding without becoming more distant, the wooden stiffness of his knees alarming him.

Do you know what I got you two? said Maureen. Nothing. Nothing at all. April Fools.

He wanted to rub his knees but he could not make his hands loosen their grip on the steering wheel.

Eric crestfallen, childish. April foolish.

Of wounds, she sang. And healing wounds.

And he feeling the dizziness caused by the motion of the car speeding backwards. The smell of the mid-green latex paint in his nose.

Okay, okay, Eric, he said. Okay.

He did not know how the animal had gotten into the car. Its presence was not unwelcome. It was a prickly creature, the size of a hat, with a white tail and no apparent legs. He was not sure if there was one or several of them because, although they appeared in many places, on the dash, on the seat beside him, on the floor, wherever he looked in fact, he never saw two at the same time.

Okay, Eric, he said. So I didn't understand that of all the many things, the many things, Eric, you have given me, that was, it was, yes the most valuable, Eric, your suffering, your hard-sell ranting, the gift, as Maureen put it, you made us, the gift of the cry of a heart overthrown, as she put it on the phone to me, you recognize her style I know.

The animal was attempting to climb up his wooden shins, but repeatedly slipped around to the underside of his legs, and dropped off. This was not unpleasant.

And that was the last I heard from her before she got on her plane for Pittsburgh or wherever, no one will tell me. And you coaching in Lisbon, browbeating Portuguese no doubt with your Irish accent.

Remember the waiter, Eric? The waiter who laughed at his own crippled English, and caressed his little nipple, as brown and round as a Canadian cent.

And then there's me, thanks to the two of you, exiled in the same raw, tearswept town I can't stay in and I can't leave.

Ah, but why oh why, Eric, did I never show you how to count up to a thousand on your fingers, nine hundred and ninety, actually. Or manage to make you see the runner running beside me on the outside. Why did I never tell you that the reason I won the Calypso was because there was an apple on the track, a red and yellow apple in mint condition on the inside lane, from first lap to last, seven runners and none of us ever kicked it away, no official from anywhere ever came and picked it up, so that as the race progressed my curiosity was just pulling me along, all I could think about was the apple and whether it would still be there the next time around, and it was, thanks be to whomever, otherwise I would have finished fourth. The apple never failed me, Eric.

What I wouldn't do to forget the night in Rotterdam. The best moments are too sad to remember.

I must say I'm cold though. My knees are turning to wood. My hands are glued to the wheel but I can't see it raining too much.

I'm training too much. Counting steps by the thousand. Spending my time waiting for time to go by.

The animal was sitting on his shoulder. Perhaps there had been several after all and they had grown together, for it was now much larger. Its tail, if it had been white, was black now and it had a long snout. It decided to move to the other shoulder, and the coldness of the animal as it passed over his face so took his breath away that he could not speak for a time.

So Maureen, as I say, jumped on a plane to Baltimore or somewhere, maybe you know where, nobody will tell me. So I won't see her again, and I won't see you again, and you won't see her and she won't see me and we won't see each other and so on and so on and on and on.

The animal climbed over his face onto the other shoulder. But no sooner had it settled there, then it decided to change shoulders again. With each pass, the animal drew its bristly white tail over his mouth, the weight of the tail forcing open his lips.

I'm running into the heartache and the thousand.

The coldness of the tail as it dropped into his mouth made him writhe.

You've left me, Maureen. With ice in my hair. Deserted me, defected me. You're gone and forgetting.

There was ice in his eyes.

I'm dying in the last lap, Eric, I am. There's not a single wriggling soul breathing beside me.

He blinked away the ice in his eyes, but it reformed immediately. He blinked again, but he could not blink fast enough, the ice was growing, freezing his eyes, they were becoming hard and slippery, rolling in their sockets.

When suddenly his body lurched into wakefulness. He grabbed the key and turned it hard in the ignition. He pumped the accelerator. The engine barely moaned as the flickering headlights faded away altogether. He released the key and turned it again, but this time the engine was silent.

He sat back.

He was shivering with cold but he was quite refreshed.

He was so awake now that he was clearly separated from all he had been dreaming.

And so he got out of the car and made his way back through the mud to where the boards lead to the new sports complex. He sat down on the boards, took off his boots, put on his running shoes, and started out.

Four-five-six-seven.

Counting his strides methodically each time his left foot touched the ground.

Fourteen-fifteen.

Thinking, I'll be home, at this pace, in eighty-five or ninety minutes.

Running easily through the night.

Thinking, I won't forget you. Not ever. What time is it in Portugal, anyway?

Running.

Into the glare of the nylon curtains.

In the dead light.

Where she sang.

SEE THE RIVER LIT UP WITH TEARS

It was pouring snow. So much so that Evelyn, who was breathing hard through her mouth, choked when she inhaled. She strained and jerked at Fairhead's wheelchair, barely tall enough to see over his bandaged head.

Millions of white insects, she thought. An infestation of snow. The disease it carries will melt into my hair. I will have sores behind my ears with scabs that crack open.

"Starboard fifteen!" sang out Fairhead. "Starboard twenty! Hard to starboard, quartermaster!"

He made sounds in his throat like explosions, collisions, crashings of waves, as the wheelchair lurched in the slush like a frightened, wet animal.

"What is the victim's name?" said the inspector.

"Fairhead. Richard, or Ralph, Fairhead," said the officer.

"Richard *or* Ralph?"

"Richard according to the name on his shirt collar. Ralph according to what's written in his shoes. No other ID. He was found unconscious in his wheelchair last night around 11:30 not far from the laundromat where he allegedly works. He had suffered a severe blow to the head and various minor injuries to the face and upper body. And of course it was very cold out, so he was cold. There were no witnesses."

"He's all right?"

"Apparently. He spent the night at Saint Michael's. They checked him out this morning and brought him here. He doesn't respond to questioning. He doesn't say anything at all."

"We won't be able to do much for him if he doesn't say anything."

Evelyn tried the front doors to the market. They were open. She stumbled back to the sidewalk to get Fairhead, the snow so cold in her eyebrows her head ached. She pulled at the wheelchair, dragged it backwards to the doors, managed to wrench it over the threshold and inside. She was breathing so heavily now she could not stand up straight.

This confined air, she thought, has been into hundreds of red lungs, rubbed itself against any number of coughing, shiny faces without ever getting out. It will push its stringy white roots into me and make me sick. She stamped and beat her arms.

Fairhead rolled himself down a short ramp that cut through the three or four stairs to the foyer. The concrete floor was covered with black patches of flattened chewing gum. The inner doors were locked, the market behind them deserted.

The foyer was full of echo, and Fairhead sang out several big notes to find the most resonant.

"Leave me here," he said. "There's just the two of us, you and me, and you know I can't be trusted."

"If you think I'm afraid of you," said Evelyn. "You're not mean just because you say you are. Not even because you tried to have at me once with your big thing sticking out."

"Evelyn," said Fairhead, "I'm sorry. I am. I don't know what . . . forgive me."

"I came and got you, didn't I?"

"I don't know what came over me. It was like some other liquid in my veins. Much faster than blood."

"And right there behind the kitchen where anyone might have heard us, if they hadn't all been eating up their pork chops in the cafeteria. What would they have said if they'd seen us? But they all still think you're sincere and big-hearted."

"We know what I really am."

"One of us knows."

Fairhead looked at Evelyn. The damp, she thought, feeling her wet, flat hair, the damp makes tiny bubbles in your skin, each bubble a swarm of licking mites.

"Don't look at me," she said.

"I was just wondering who it is," said Fairhead, "who lights such a fire in me one day, such a fire, and who is, at the same time, on such close terms with fate that the very next day I should be thumped unconscious for my actions."

"Tell me what happened, Fairhead," said Evelyn. "Did they hurt you?"

"I never saw them. I closed the laundromat as I do at eleven, a little after maybe. I went trundling down Regent Street and there they were, walking behind me on each side. I could just see their breath out of the corner of my eye. They scuffed along, kicking my wheels, not saying anything, giggling. And then, it was as if the cold air snapped its fingers with a big snap, and they had at me."

"Ayee," said Evelyn.

"Pfff," said Fairhead. "I woke up in the hospital with this bandage, like a white squash on my head. They took me to the police station this morning. And then you came."

"Did they wash your head well?" said Evelyn.

"How should I know."

"Blood is a horrible thing," she said, "when it gets out. Everything grows in blood. Millions of squealing larvas. Millions."

"Did you get in touch with the owner of the laundromat?" said the inspector.

"Yes," said the officer. "He said that Fairhead has been working there for some time, gets his mail there even, makes change, does laundry that's left, sweeps up, things somebody in a wheelchair can do, everybody likes him, good PR. He says he's very happy with him, wouldn't know why anyone would want to harm him. He got him through Social Services, the government pays his salary."

"He still hasn't said anything?"

"Not a word."

"And the people at the hospital are sure he's okay?"

"He looks okay."

"He looks okay," said the inspector. "I *look* okay. If he doesn't pipe up soon, send him home."

"Home," said the officer.

Evelyn examined the mealy efflorescence on the cement wall. She could see it growing. The temptation to plunge her finger into it made her heart race, to feel the blood of the wall spurt onto her mouth.

"Tell me again, Fairhead," she said, "what happened to your legs. If you like."

"How did I lose the use of my legs?" said Fairhead. "You see, I used to be an architect once. I walked everywhere. I wore a purple hat with a brim that was very wide on one side. I had a red beard then.

"I went to the Malagasy Republic to show the people how to build stronger homes. They drove me around in a corrugated car, but they didn't like me. Their children crowded around me, screeching and whining, putting their hands in all my pockets. And they just went on building their homes out of straw and quicklime, as they always had.

"So I decided to go to the highlands, to Antananarivo. My guide was a Malgache woman. It was hard climbing. The Malgache woman rubbed my legs with vanilla to strengthen them. And then, one night, she left me.

"I went on alone, exhausted and very hungry, until at last I came to a village.

"The village chief took me in. His daughter was not healthy, she suffered from incontinence and bled. She talked all the time with her jagged teeth, and she always looked at me when she talked, even if I walked behind her.

"Her father was not happy when he learned she was in love with me. He locked me in a small hut and brought me my meals himself. He watched me eat, talked to me, taught me many details of their language.

"He told me that he wanted to build a big house. He described all the rooms and their dimensions, as so many "standing men" long and so many "standing men" wide. He could not count beyond six or seven. After that he resorted to "many," "little many," "big many," and so on. He would bring men villagers, stand them at arms' length one from another and say "that many," and I would write down the number. He constantly asked for my assurance that it would be possible to build such a big house. I answered that I did not see why not. And when one day he asked with extreme earnestness if a second story could be constructed, I said, "A second, and even a third." And he was very happy.

"So I set about gathering tea-tree twigs which I glued together to make an exact model of the house. I devoted many days to the building of this model and was very proud of it. I made the people understand that every twig represented a padauk board, and that the house must be constructed exactly as the model was, or it would fall down.

"Several weeks were spent felling padauk trees, cutting boards, and making wooden dowels and nails. And then, amid great excitement, the construction was begun. Every morning I put on my purple, wide-brimmed hat and stepped out of my hut to supervise the day's work, and every evening the father led me back to my hut with my supper in his hands, talked to me while I ate, and admired my model.

"In the end, the house was very well constructed, and finished with considerable skill.

"I had made the outside walls of the house two feet wide. The inner and outer surfaces of these walls were tied together by a large number of horizontal boards in a seemingly haphazard pattern. In fact, I had planned the position of these tie-boards very carefully when making my model, and had assured myself that their position was duplicated exactly during construction.

"As well, each bedroom was provided with a toilet, that is to say, a privy hole. The matter from these privies merely dropped into a ditch that had been dug between the inner and outer walls, and that drained towards an outlet at the lowest corner.

"This outlet was just large enough for me to crawl through. Once inside the walls, it was not difficult, despite the darkness, to scale the horizontal tie-boards because, as I say, I knew exactly where they were. And so I climbed up to the daughter's room, and entered through the privy hole.

"She was not astonished to see me. She had been waiting. She was not astonished, not overjoyed.

"Every night I visited her, and she was very happy.

"When her father learned that she was still in love with me, he made a fire. He made a fire and sat me in front of it with my purple hat, and sang long songs to me. When he sang softly the fire burned softly, and when he sang loudly, the fire whipped and spat.

"And when he had finished, he picked me up in his own arms and set me on the back of the strongest man. Because I could no longer walk."

"Has he said anything?" said the inspector.

"No," said the officer. "I spoke to the head honcho at Social Services, the head honcha. Got quite excited when she heard that Fairhead had been roughed up, said we better find the perpetrators who did it. The only address she has for him is the laundromat. Apart from that, she said he's at Social Services quite a bit, eats at the cafeteria, helps out sometimes at the mental health clinic."

"He's a crackerjack," said the inspector.

"Not the impression I got. He just helps out. I told her he hasn't said a word since he got here. She said she didn't know why *any*body would want to talk to the police, ha ha, said she'd work on it and hung up."

"Fairhead," said Evelyn, "I want to give you this."

"What is it?" said Fairhead.

"A flashlight. Peter gave it to me."

"I don't want it if Peter gave it to you."

"Take it. I want to give you something. Take it, or I won't have the courage anymore."

"But what will your *fiancé* say?" said Fairhead.

"Peter's not my fiancé. Not really. He knows me. He'll give me something else."

She put the flashlight into Fairhead's hand. Fairhead shone the flashlight under his chin so that the beam threw cheap shadows on his face, and his bandage looked as though it were made of glass.

"I can feel that the flashlight has been in your hand," he said. The shadows on his face bounced with the movements of his lips. "That it has been in your pocket. That while it was in your pocket it rubbed against you, there." He directed the beam onto Evelyn's coat, saying, "There! And there!" The beam played all over Evelyn who did not flinch.

Fairhead shone the flashlight then for several seconds directly into his own open eyes, after which he squeezed them shut so hard his nose crinkled, and his teeth were bared.

"Look at all the shadows squirm," he said. "Whew. I see . . . I see the ghost of a pig running. A blue, dripping pig."

And still Evelyn could feel the flashlight beam nestling into her neck, feel it burrowing through the fabric of her coat, nosing its way under her collar and up her sleeves. The light crawled over her shoulders and down her back, licking off every brown growth and mole. Do not move, she said to herself. Do not move, and it won't bite you.

"Don't hate Peter," she said softly.

"And why not!" said Fairhead.

The skin of her back was open and red from the licking of the light. It grated against her clothing as she breathed in and out. Don't be afraid, she said to herself. Don't move. Don't breathe even. But she breathed all the faster, and the faster she breathed, the more the light licked.

"Don't hate him because he wants to marry me."

"I hate him because you want to marry *him*."

The points of the light's teeth pricked into Evelyn. Her

skin was burning, like infant skin. It will bite me, she thought, if I move, if I move. If I stroke it. It won't bite me if I stroke it. It will like me.

"Don't hate Peter," she said. "It hurts me."

"You brought it up," said Fairhead. "Why do you make me show off my scars to you? Why do you want to look? Go. Leave me alone here, and don't ask any more. I have his flashlight at least."

She tried to stroke the light but it licked her all the faster. It pushed its small snout between her legs, snuffled at her excitedly, made wounded noises in its throat. It started to bite.

"You make me afraid," she said desperately.

"Go then. Go. Go."

"Fairhead," she whimpered, "I need to go to the toilet."

"Well go then," said Fairhead.

"I can't." She was crying now. "It will bite me. It will."

"Bite you!" shouted Fairhead. "*I'll* bite you."

His voice rushed at Evelyn, struck her on the chest with such force that she stumbled backwards.

But the light did not bite her. It likes me, she thought. It does. She hurried into a corner, giddy with relief.

"Don't look at my bum," she said cheerfully.

"I'm not going to look," said Fairhead.

"You can if you like. I don't mind. I've already seen some of your bum, haven't I? Just some, when I helped you put your pants back on. Peter never lets me look. He doesn't want me to see his big thing. I'll show you my thing if you like. I've already seen yours, haven't I? I'll say I have. Look, Fairhead, look. Woo woo. Look, Fairhead. I don't mind. You can look. Fairhead! Look! That's better. See? That's my little thing. Woo-oo. I don't know why," she said, putting her underwear back on, "I was so frightened. I like you. I do."

She sat down beside the wheelchair.

"I do like you, Fairhead."

"Go now," said Fairhead.

"Tell me again," she said, "if you like, how you lost your legs."

"The head honcha is sending somebody over," said the officer. "To get Fairhead. A girl who knows him, an outpatient."

"Another crackerjack you mean," said the inspector.

The officer grunted. "At any rate, she's going to come and pick him up. The head honcha says she'll pay for the taxi one way, but that we have to pay the fare back to her place."

The inspector grunted. "He still hasn't said anything?"

"Nothing at all."

"Make sure he gets the full taxi allowance then, whatever it is now."

"Thirty-two fifty-eight," said the officer.

"Make sure he gets that then."

"How did I lose the use of my legs?" said Fairhead. "When I was young, I lived on the Saint Croix River. There were many islands in the river where no one lived, some wooded, some bare rock. The birds were very plentiful on these islands, gulls and terns, cormorants, shearwaters. Petrels sometimes. And several seasons in a row, a bald eagle built its nest high up in a dying fir on the edge of one of the wooded islands. Every day, small boats and launches passed by, bristling with sightseers, their binoculars trained on the nest.

"My cousin was almost my age. Her feet were so big she wore her mother's shoes, she had thin eyes, and her brown, toasted hair reminded me all winter long of the hot days in August. We were always together. She punched me whenever she didn't win, and screamed when I punched her.

"One summer, we decided to steal the eggs from the eagle's nest. We went out in her father's aluminum boat and beached it on the far side of the island. When we got to the fir tree, the eagle was there above us, flapping away awkwardly, as though the nest were very hot to the touch. And then he flew off in his heavy, indolent way.

"It was not a difficult tree to climb, not even particularly tall. Nor was the nest as large as I had thought it would be, although, I suppose, it was nearly half as big as I was. There were three eggs inside, one that was fat and speckled, two that were dull grey and much smaller.

"We looked at each other, and I shot my hand into the nest. But no sooner had I taken hold of the big egg, then bang! the entire tree twisted and trembled. The eagle, in his clumsy desperation, had crashed into it too high, his wings were tangled in the crowd of dying branches, enormous, cracked, heaving wings, as black and chipped as iron.

"I was terrified. I pushed the egg into my mouth and started down, slipping from branch to branch, bouncing, falling. I could hear my cousin squealing above me, not in fear, but in pain, in anger, she was furious, the eagle was on her, and she, I know, was after the other eggs.

"We struck the ground almost at the same instant, almost together. She called to me, but I, she was dying, you see, her brown head was full of blood, but I, I was not even hurt. No no my legs were fine. I was not hurt and she called to me, but I, you see the egg broke in my mouth, I swallowed the slimy, living thing in the egg, and it made me puke.

"And she was dying.

"I couldn't let them know that I wasn't even hurt. I told them I couldn't feel my legs. They howled and cried and carried on. I don't know how I did it, all that time, always making my legs be floppy and stupid, when all I wanted was to stand up and run.

"They turned the island into a sanctuary after that and named it after my cousin. They asked for donations from all the birdwatchers until they had enough to buy me my first wheelchair.

"I still get out of my wheelchair sometimes. My legs are very weak now. But I get out sometimes. I'll show you, if you like. Help me."

Evelyn did not move. After a time, she said, "Fairhead, I know you do not want me to feel sorry and say poor Fairhead. I am so happy. Too happy. But I want you to know that I don't think less of you because of what you tried to do to me. Or what you are. None of us do. You are our friend, Fairhead. I say so, and it's true."

"Pfff," said Fairhead.

"Ugly," said the officer. "You should have seen her. She couldn't have been five feet tall. She could barely see over the wheelchair. And ugly. Fat. And not just fat but you know with that clotted, fatty look. And this tiny head. Like a giant flea."

"I think I get the idea," said the inspector.

"Right out of dreamland. Right out of it. She wanted me to change the air in the tires of the wheelchair. She thought there were insects growing in them that would bite her if the tires leaked. Peter, she said, puts fresh air in my tires every day."

"Peter?" said the inspector. "I thought his name was Richard or Ralph."

"I don't know," said the officer. "I don't know if Richard or Ralph's pump can put fresh air in anybody's tires. Anyway, I managed to convince her that the tires were solid rubber."

"And you put them in a taxi, did you?" said the inspector.

"I gave Fairhead the thirty-two fifty-eight and told them to call themselves a taxi at the reception desk."

"Evelyn," said Fairhead, "I love you."

"Ooh," said Evelyn, "you certainly made it clear that you love me! Pointing your big thing at me. Woo-oo. But I'm too quick for you."

"Anybody is quicker than a stone," said Fairhead, pouting. "It isn't easy for me, Evelyn. Living, lifeless."

"I know, Fairhead. But what do you want from me?"

"You! I want you!"

"But I am yours. I am everybody's. Think, Fairhead, if I'd let you have what you wanted, would you be more happy now?"

"Pfff," said Fairhead.

"I am just Evelyn. I have my friends, I have my car, and I have Peter. That's all. There is no more. I am so happy, Fairhead. Too happy."

She put her hands on each side of Fairhead's neck and kissed him on the mouth.

"I can't stay here anymore," she said.

"Go then," said Fairhead. "Go on. I won't see you again, ever."

"Yes you will. You're coming with me." She took hold of the wheelchair by the handles.

She groaned as she tried to push Fairhead up the ramp. But Fairhead, in order to stop her, grabbed the tires hard. This so surprised Evelyn, that she lost her balance, the wheelchair tipped over backwards and to one side, knocking her down.

"Look what you've done!" yelled Fairhead, as the money from his pockets rattled away. "Get me up! Get me up!"

His voice rushed into Evelyn's ears, swelling the nerves in her forehead, stiffening her veins so that she could not move. She gathered her face into a tight knot to prevent herself from crying.

"Do not scream at me," she tried to say, but her voice was a wet finger deep in her throat. Fairhead tried to right himself, lunging spasmodically like a rawboned, gooey chick, half-hatched from an unyielding egg. The egg merely grated along the floor, making white scratches.

"Inspector," said the officer.

"Yes."

"The head honcha phoned to say Fairhead and the girl haven't arrived yet. Very sarcastic."

"So."

"It's snowing."

"It snows in the winter."

"It's snowing hard."

"It snows hard in the winter."

"Christine, at reception? seems to think that Fairhead and the girl maybe didn't get in a taxi after all. She definitely didn't call them one. She didn't see them get into one."

The two men looked at each other for several seconds.

"Get your coat," said the inspector.

"There is a pulse in the ground," said Evelyn. "The earth beats." She sat, very tired, her arms trembling, beside Fairhead in his overturned wheelchair. She had tried and tried, but she had not been able to get him up. "The heart in a stone beats only once every three hundred years. But even so, every stone's heart has beaten more than yours and mine together, Fairhead. A stone can break open with the beat of its own heart. It can let out a puff of poison air as old as when there were just fish. Or when fish were men, I forget. It doesn't matter. Be careful of stones, Fairhead. Our lungs cannot breathe their air. Smell them. Sometimes they creak, sometimes they stumble, sometimes they snatch at you."

"Listen, Fairhead," she said, "the ground around us is beating on the walls. Listen."

"Don't go," said Fairhead.

"The walls cannot hold forever, Fairhead, the ground will break in sometime. Look, already there are these white, running scabs on the walls. The earth is full of beetles with shiny teeth so long they can't close their mouths, full of worms wrapped up in foam. They only have to touch you, Fairhead. They only have to make their little wriggling caca in your hair once. Just once."

"Shhhh," said Fairhead. "Shhhh."

"Ha!" said Evelyn. "If you think you can shut them up."

"Don't go," said Fairhead. "Don't go."

"I can smell them. The littlest ones are here already. You can't see them. But they smell. They smell like candies burning. Scream at them, Fairhead. Scream at them."

"Don't, Evelyn."

"Scream at them."

"Don't go, Evelyn. It isn't any better outside. You know that. Look, there is all this new snow now. It will shine the sunlight into your eyes so that they turn white."

"That isn't even true," said Evelyn. "Besides, my eyes are strong."

"Don't go," said Fairhead. "Look what's outside. Look, you can see the sidewalks that crumble under your very feet, can't you? You can see the schoolbuses lying on their backs, silent, the tires still spinning. Look, Evelyn. The streets are melting away, dripping like blood into the river, the sky is so hard you can see how the birds break their wings on it, you can see them cry, you can see the river lit up with tears. You can't go. I'll tell you how I lost my legs."

"I used to be a truck driver," he said, for he dared not stop talking. "I've been in every province. I drove in the winter from Winnipeg to Lynn Lake, carrying prefabricated wall frames. 613 miles, most of it empty wilderness. 50 below, 75 often. I'd turn up the heater until I was fairly french-fried, and just drive and drive. By the time I got to Lundar, my feet would be so hot I had to take my boots off. By Ashern I had taken off my shoes. And from St. Martin Junction on, I drove barefoot.

“I was so hot I was almost glad to open the door to relieve myself. I used to shout at the cold, my voice turning into a puff of ice. I shouted at the cold the way children shout at sleeping bears in cages. And then I’d get in and slam the door.

“I had got as far as Paint Lake, and I had to piss. I opened the door and shouted away. But then, when I was nearly finished, I pushed myself out you see, so I wouldn’t dribble onto the truck, and I lost my balance. I just lost my balance and fell out of the truck. I didn’t even fall out, because I caught hold of the door. But my right foot touched the running board you see, the little toe and the one beside it, that’s all, the two toes just touched the metal running board. And stuck there.

“I couldn’t pull them off, could I.

“I couldn’t pull them off.

“So I chewed them off.

“Didn’t I.

“It was the only way. But to chew them off you see, I had to let go the door. I had to put my other foot in the snow.

“And still I drove to Thompson, although the sound of my little bones cracking between my own teeth was a dream frozen in my ears.

“In Thompson they put me on a plane to Winnipeg. The cold inside me woke up on the airplane and began to shout back. It screamed in every part of me, screaming and screaming until the co-pilot put a sock in my mouth to shut it up.”

“That isn’t even true,” said Evelyn, standing up.

“I saw my feet,” said Fairhead, “before they lopped them off. They tried to prevent me, but I saw them. They were as black and mushy as old bananas. All except where I'd kept the right one warm chewing off my toes."

"That isn't even true," said Evelyn. "There is no girl in that story. And anyway, you have feet. I've seen them. You just want to make me frightened. I'm leaving you, Fairhead."

But Fairhead had already taken hold of Evelyn's ankle, and twisting it, he forced her back down onto the floor.

"I'm leaving," she said, not even resisting.

He got her boots off, and one shoe.

"I was happy," he said, "until I met you. It didn't matter if I was what I am."

He held her white foot. "You're the one," he said. "You are." He opened his mouth and made to bite into her toes. But Evelyn, who still had not resisted, turned over so suddenly that Fairhead lost his grip. She got up quickly and snatched her boots away before he could grab them.

"It didn't matter!" he screamed. "You're the one who made me what I am. It's you, it's you, it's you. You pig. You fat, dripping pig!"

But Evelyn already had her boots on. He heard the scuffing sound of her footsteps on the stairs. He heard the bang of the metal bar as the door was opened, heard the murmur out of doors for a long moment.

"Don't, Evelyn," he said to himself.

He heard the latch click shut.

"Don't go."

"*Mis*ter Fairhead!" said the inspector, squinting into the foyer after the brightness of the snow outside, the eagerness in his voice caused both by his relief at finding Fairhead, and by his alarm at finding him in such dire straits. He jumped down the steps in a single bound, righted the wheelchair, and looked intently into Fairhead's face.

"Are you all right? Are you hurt? . . . You didn't get too very far, did you? Heavy going in the snow I guess, eh, but at least you left a good trail. Even a police inspector can follow wheelchair tracks. So you're okay?"

The officer, for his part, gathered up the scattered money, bending deeply at the knees to lower his massive body. He sniffed indifferently at the puddle of urine, picked up the flashlight, stuffed it and the money into a pocket of the inspector's coat, as the inspector continued to scrutinize Fairhead.

"So," said the inspector. "The girl go for help, did she? We didn't see her. I'm the inspector by the way, we haven't met, but the officer has told me about you."

"Well now," he said, "what'll we do with you? For starters, I think we'll take you back to the police station, and after that, we'll just see, eh? We'll just see. So, just let me. I don't think we'll bother trying to push you through the snow."

He slid his hands under Fairhead's arms and lifted him out.

"Now then, Mr. Fairhead," he said, "I'm going to put you on the officer's back. If you'll just put your arms around his neck, good, and he'll take you under the legs. Any problem with that? Comfortable? Your bandage is all . . . why don't we just take it off, it'll heal faster anyway. So. You've got your scarf and your gloves, and I've got your money I guess, okay, and I've got *my* money, and I'll take the wheelchair, we're not leaving anything behind, are we?"

"I assure you, Mr. Fairhead," said the inspector, banging the metal bar to open the door for them, "the officer's not going to drop you. He's the strongest man we've got."

"On the back," said Fairhead, "of the strongest man."

The officer hesitated, but Fairhead said nothing more. He stepped outside then past the inspector, turning his head as he did so, saying, silently, with exaggerated movements of his lips: "He's crying."